Welcome to the Secret World of Alex Mack!

The new year brings a lot of changes. This year, I've decided to act more grown-up and rely less on my powers. Paradise Valley is changing, too. Mr. Dobbs, CEO of a large manufacturing company, wants to bring his business here. It'll bring in more jobs *and* take power away from Danielle Atron. Most of the town is excited, but I'm a little suspicious. The deal seems too good to be true. I want to find out the truth, but is it worth using my powers? Let me explain. . . .

I'm Alex Mack. I was just another average kid until my first day of junior high.

One minute I'm walking home from school—the next there's a *crash!* A truck from the Paradise Valley Chemical plant overturns in front of me, and I'm drenched in some weird chemical.

And since then—well, nothing's been the same. I can move objects with my mind, shoot electrical charges through my fingertips, and morph° into a liquid shape . . . which is handy when I get in a tight spot!

My best friend, Ray, thinks it's cool—and my sister, Annie, thinks I'm a science project.

They're the only two people who know about my new powers. I can't let anyone else find out—not even my parents—because I know the chemical plant wants to find me and turn me into some experiment.

But you know something? I guess I'm not so average anymore!

The Secret World of Alex Mack™

Available from MINSTREL Books

the secret world of

ALEX MACK™

New Year's Revolution!

Diana G. Gallagher

A MINSTREL® BOOK

Published by POCKET BOOKS
New York   London   Toronto   Sydney   Tokyo   Singapore

A MINSTREL PAPERBACK *Original*

A Minstrel Book published by
POCKET BOOKS, a division of Simon & Schuster Inc.
1230 Avenue of the Americas, New York, NY 10020

ISBN: 0-671-01555-9

First Minstrel Books printing December 1997

10 9 8 7 6 5 4 3 2 1

Cover photography by Pat Hill Studio, Thomas Queally, and Danny Feld

Printed in the U.S.A.

For Monica Sehgal,
a talented young artist
and very special friend

New Year's Revolution!

CHAPTER 1

Sitting on the couch in the living room, Alex sighed. A pen dangled in midair before her, held in place by the telekinetic force of her GC-161-enhanced mind. A spiral notebook lay open on her lap. No sound disturbed the silence in the empty house and no inspired thought broke the surface of her absentminded daze. With its brightly blinking lights dimmed by the afternoon sun streaming through the window, even the Christmas tree mirrored her gloomy mood.

Alex sighed again. The silver, gold, red, green, and blue packages that had overflowed the corner around the tree were gone, ripped open to delighted squeals of surprise and polite mur-

murs of guarded disappointment two days ago. Only a bundle of sports socks, a personalized, leather-bound organizer Annie had given her, and an assortment of impractical kitchen gadgets everyone in the Mack family had purchased from Louis Driscoll's father remained, unsettling reminders that she could no longer use the excitement of the approaching holiday as an excuse.

The essay was due the day she went back to school after Christmas break.

The pen dropped to the floor as Alex shifted her gaze and her concentration to the blue-lined page on her knees.

A blank page.

Like her mind.

"And my life!" Throwing the notebook over her shoulder with her hand, Alex picked up and threw the pen with a powerful, frustrated thought. It hit the far wall with a sharp crack, fell onto the table, and rolled toward the edge. Telekinetically retrieving it, she whisked it back across the room and into her hand, then calmed herself with a deep breath.

Losing my temper isn't going to get the assignment written, Alex reflected dismally. But, she wasn't making much progress staying calm, either.

Thinking the notebook off the floor and onto her lap, she wrote:

MY CAREER CHOICE FOR THE TWENTY-FIRST CENTURY

Gripping the pen with renewed determination, Alex chewed on the plastic end as she tried to decide how to begin. After two minutes of intense thought, she had to admit that trying to write anything was hopeless because she didn't know what to write about.

The awful truth was that she didn't have a clue what she wanted to do with her life—beyond getting the short but difficult essay done and handed in on time.

Since taking notes always seemed to stimulate her brain, Alex flipped to another page. "Talents and aptitudes," she said aloud as she quickly scribbled a list. "Telekinesis. Turn into a liquid. Create instant electrical charges—"

"What?" Annie asked as she came in from the kitchen with a glass of milk and a handful of cookies.

"What?" Startled, Alex jumped.

In the few months her brilliant older sister had been away at college, Alex had gotten used to *not* having her coming and going all the time. Home on Christmas break, Annie had settled back in as though she had never been gone. Alex didn't mind having to share the bedroom again for a couple of weeks or fighting over whose preference in music the other had to tolerate. She had missed Annie a lot more than she had thought she would, and it wasn't just because her genius sister was always helping her out of the jams her amazing powers got her into. Over the years, since her genetic structure had been altered by the top-secret experimental compound GC-161 in a Paradise Valley Chemical truck accident, they had become close friends, too. But Annie's unexpected popping in and out was wreaking havoc on her nerves.

"I asked you first." Perching on the end of the couch, Annie bit a vanilla wafer in half and leaned over to glance at the notebook.

"I didn't hear you come in." Defensively snatching the notebook away from Annie's prying eyes, Alex scowled. "I *really* wish you wouldn't sneak up on me like that. My heart's still pounding double-time."

Unperturbed, Annie washed the cookie down with a sip of milk. "Got a big problem, huh?"

"No, I—" Touched by Annie's insight, Alex

nodded and handed her the notebook. "Yeah. You could say that."

" 'Talents and aptitudes,' " Annie mumbled. "Is this one of those 'what I want to be when I grow up' assignments?"

"In five hundred words, but at the rate I'm going it might as well be a million."

Puzzled, Annie frowned. "It's only a couple of pages."

Alex shrugged. "But I don't have any ideas."

Scooting back, Annie curled her legs under her. "Well, let's see. Telekinesis. That has some interesting possibilities. If you were a librarian you wouldn't need a ladder to reach the top shelves to put books back."

"As long as no one was looking," Alex agreed with an amused grin.

"Or—" Annie's eyes brightened as she gained momentum. "If you were a plumber, you could just morph to check out clogged pipes or find rings and things your customers dropped down the drain!"

"I don't think so." Wrinkling her nose, Alex responded in the spirit of fun Annie intended. "Too dark and damp, and *way* too claustrophobic."

"How about Alex Mack's Road Service?"

Annie lowered her voice and mimicked a typical radio announcer. "No cables needed to jump-start your car!"

"Rent a human glow-stick for your kids on Halloween!" Alex laughed, then sobered suddenly. "This is serious, Annie. The essay is just the first part of a college and career study we're doing next semester."

Nodding, Annie's expression grew serious, too. "I remember. It's part of the curriculum for every freshman class. But don't worry about it, okay? It's a snap."

"For you, maybe." Exhaling with disgust, Alex slouched back against the couch. A scientific genius like their father, Annie had never questioned her prospects for the future. "You've always known you wanted to be a superscientist who wins the Nobel prize. I don't have a clue."

"So make something up. It's not like you have to make an ironclad commitment to your life's work in a few paragraphs."

"Yeah, I suppose." Alex frowned, disturbed by an uneasy feeling that went deeper than the necessity of having to fabricate a career goal for English.

"Omigosh! It's almost three!" Jumping up, Annie shoved the empty milk glass at Alex, then ran toward the stairs. "Rinse that out for me, will you? I promised Christine Michaels I'd meet her at the mall."

"The mall?" Alex gaped at her retreating sister in astonishment. To the best of her knowledge, Annie had never in her life dashed off to the bustling center of commercial enterprise that attracted most of Paradise Valley's teenagers. "Why are you going to the mall?"

Stopping halfway up the stairs, Annie looked back. "Why do most people go there?"

"To shop."

"Right. If I don't want to spend the next few months running around campus in rags or naked, I've got to get a few things." Shaking her head, Annie took the rest of the stairs two at a time.

Smiling, Alex wondered if any of the local stores carried designer lab coats with color-coordinated plastic pocket protectors.

There's an idea, Alex thought as she rose and went into the kitchen with the glass. She could create a line of fashionable lab-wear for the style-conscious scientist. *Alex Mack: designer for the really brainy!* Except, she realized with a downward glance at her high-tops, jeans, and baggy sweatshirt, her own casually funky style proba-

7

bly wasn't sophisticated enough to appeal to scientists, either.

Besides, she wasn't nearly as interested in keeping up with all the latest fashion trends as most girls her age. In fact, although she had a healthy curiosity about everything, there wasn't *one* thing that had ever really captured and held her interest for long.

Sunk in the mire of that depressing revelation, Alex didn't hear her mother at the back door and jumped again when Barbara Mack banged it open.

"Give me a hand with these, Alex." Clutching two full bags of groceries, Mrs. Mack stooped slightly to stop one from slipping out of her arm.

Simultaneously rushing to assist and keeping the bag from falling with a telekinetic nudge, Alex grabbed it before the contents dumped on the floor. "You shouldn't try to carry so much at one time, Mom."

Setting the other bag on the table, Barbara nodded and blew a stray lock of blond hair off her forehead. "You're right, but I've got to change and make several calls before my four-thirty meeting with Valerie Lincoln. If I don't get started now, I'll be late," she said with a quick glance at the wall clock. "Would you put those away for me?"

"Sure." Lifting a carton of orange juice and a gallon of milk out of the bag, Alex turned toward the refrigerator. "Mom?"

"What?" Pausing in the doorway, Mrs. Mack glanced back with a slightly frazzled, questioning frown.

"Well, I was wondering what made you decide to go into public relations." Alex put the orange juice on the counter and opened the refrigerator door. "I mean, it's not exactly the kind of career a kid gets excited about. You know, like being a fireman or an astronaut or something like that—"

"Gosh, Alex, I can't. Not right now." Smiling apologetically, Mrs. Mack shrugged. "I told Valerie I'd finalize the refreshment menu with the caterer and check with the Paradise Valley Women's Auxiliary about the decorations this afternoon. We're short on help and running out of time. This meeting will probably last a couple of hours, so you're all on your own for dinner, okay?"

Nodding, Alex hid her disappointment behind an understanding smile. The city was holding a New Year's Eve gala for the town's teenagers at the Paradise Valley Community Center. Knowing that her mother was on break from her college classes and a public relations expert, too, the mayor's wife had convinced her to be on the planning committee.

"That's okay, Mom. I was just wondering."

"No problem. I'd love to talk to you about public relations work, but after I get home, okay? Right now, I've really gotta run."

As she unloaded the rest of the groceries, Alex couldn't help feel awed by her mother's energy and accomplishments. Instead of relaxing during her vacation from classes and endless homework, her mom had eagerly donated her time and expertise to Mrs. Lincoln's teen party project. Totally organized and in control, Barbara Mack was one of those people who never seemed to have a spare minute and yet always got everything done. The house and her family had never known a moment's neglect when she had been working full-time. Then, when she had been downsized out of her job with a local public relations firm, she had not taken advantage of the opportunity to slow down and take life easy for a while. Her mother had enrolled in college again to get a degree in social work.

Folding the paper bags and storing them, Alex

shook off a twinge of envy. *Mom's launching a second career, and I don't even have a first!*

Almost as bad, Alex thought despondently. All of her friends had driving interests and inclinations that were already cementing the foundations of their futures.

And that was the real problem underlying the trouble she was having writing the essay. Making up a career goal for the assignment would satisfy her English teacher, Mrs. Broderick, but it wouldn't solve the disturbing realization the assignment had forced her to confront.

What *was* she going to do when she grew up?

Sinking into a kitchen chair, Alex dropped her chin in her hands.

There was one option that would always be open to her. She could confess to Danielle Atron that she was the GC-161 accident kid the CEO of Paradise Valley Chemical had been looking for, and dedicate the rest of her life to the advancement of science—as a human lab rat.

CHAPTER 2

Too bummed to tackle the essay again just yet, Alex got up to get her socks and organizer from under the tree. Before she had gone two steps, Ray Alvarado, her best friend and next-door neighbor, was pounding on the back door and frantically calling her name.

"Alex! Hey, Alex! Are you there!"

Wondering what the emergency was, Alex rushed to the door and threw it open. Louis Driscoll was standing behind Ray, anxiously shifting from one foot to the other. "What's the matter? What happened—"

"We're late. Come on!"

Alex blinked. "Late for what?"

"I told you she forgot," Louis said.

"*Flight of Fear.* The biggest blockbuster of the season, remember?"

"Well, actually, Ray—" Alex shrugged. "I don't remember. Are you sure we made plans to go to the movies today?"

"Of course, I'm sure! I called you right after Louis and I decided—" Ray froze, then slapped his forehead. "Oh, boy. I was *going* to call you, but an important call came in for my dad and—"

"*You* forgot." Louis emphasized the point with a jab to Ray's shoulder, then he looked back at Alex. "So, are you coming or not? 'Cause if you are, we gotta go now or the line will be so long we'll never get in."

Alex didn't hesitate. Everyone else in the family was busy and the thought of sitting home alone with her unwritten English essay mocking her lack of a real career goal was too much to bear at the moment.

"I'd love to. Just let me grab my bag—"

Ray grabbed her arm. "No time. I'll buy and you can pay me back later. Let's move."

Taking a split second to grab the knit hat she had tossed on the counter the night before, Alex darted to the garage to get her bike as the boys raced to the sidewalk and mounted theirs on the run. Pedaling as fast as she could, it took her a block and a half to catch up. By then, both boys were winded enough to slow down to a reasonable but steady speed.

Even though the mall was packed with shoppers returning gifts or taking advantage of the after-Christmas sales, they arrived at the multiplex theater five minutes ahead of Ray's schedule.

"Looks like we made it." Ray grinned as they took their places at the end of the line.

"Looks like," Alex agreed. Only about thirty kids waited ahead of them, but the line was moving at a snail's pace.

"Yeah, no problem. As long as they didn't sell a hundred tickets in advance." Scowling, Louis glanced at his watch. "Fifteen minutes to go. If this line doesn't start to move faster soon, we'll miss the opening credits. And then I'm really gonna be upset."

"Stop worrying, Louis. You're starting to sound like Robyn." Ray winked at Alex.

Alex choked back a laugh. One of her other closest friends, Robyn Russo was the ultimate pessimist who always expected the worst to happen. She could find a storm cloud in a clear blue sky.

Louis wasn't amused. "Robyn wouldn't sue. I would."

Ray started slightly. "Sue who for what?"

"The theater!" Louis flared. "For failing to provide the *whole* movie! We got here in plenty of time and we're going to pay the full price for a ticket, right?"

"Right," Alex and Ray agreed in bewildered unison.

"It's not our fault the line is moving at a speed well below average, is it?"

Ray shook his head. "No, but—"

"And *why* is the line moving slower than we should reasonably expect?" Eyes narrowing, Louis shifted his piercing gaze between the two of them.

"I don't know." Alex shrugged, intrigued by the sharp-witted boy's unusually serious demeanor. She hated missing the opening credits, too, especially since so many films began with the action rolling underneath them. But Louis's reaction to something that hadn't yet happened was more than a little extreme.

Louis rubbed his chin thoughtfully. "Perhaps, the ticket-dispensing machine is malfunctioning. Or maybe the cashier is just slow counting out change. Either way—" He raised his finger for dramatic effect. "We—the consumers—will not be at fault if we don't make it to our seats before the movie begins."

"Right!" Ray frowned, still confused. "So?"

"So we should be entitled to a full refund." Crossing his arms, Louis smiled. "Do I have a solid case, or what?"

"Case?" Alex looked at him askance. "As in court case?"

"Exactly. I've definitely decided I want to be an attorney, but not what kind. Criminal law is exciting, but the big bucks are in corporate."

"You? A lawyer?" Ray laughed.

"What's so funny?" Louis asked.

"Actually, I thought his argument was pretty good, Ray," Alex said. She didn't add that at least Louis had some idea of what he wanted to do with his life, which was more than she could say.

"No, I agree. The argument was great, but—"

"But what, Ray?" Louis demanded.

"You're just too honest to be an attorney." Gripping Louis's shoulder, Ray sighed.

"I'll get over it." A mischievous smirk brightened Louis's face. "So what's your chosen profession this week, Ray?"

Nothing escapes Louis, Alex thought. Although

he was relatively new in town, it hadn't taken him long to realize that Ray changed his mind about what he wanted to be on a regular basis. It had started in kindergarten when he decided driving an ice cream truck was the best of all possible jobs. Since then, it had become a running joke that Ray just accepted and shrugged off.

"Actually, I've given that a lot of thought since Mrs. Broderick assigned the career essay, and there's no question." Ray hesitated.

Alex and Louis both leaned forward expectantly.

"What?" Louis asked finally.

"Wall Street and high finance."

"Now who's kidding?" Louis quipped.

Alex could tell from Ray's expression that he was serious, and held back her own comments. Sooner or later he *would* figure out what he really wanted to do and stick to it. Until then, he wasn't afraid to explore all the hundreds of exciting career possibilities. One of them would be the right one.

"What makes you think I can't be a financier?" Ray asked Louis defensively.

"You're just not ruthless enough, Ray. Sorry."

"I'll learn." Grinning, Ray turned to Alex. "What about you?"

"Me? Oh, well—I thought—" Anxious to change the subject before she blurted out something totally stupid or had to admit she just didn't know, Alex diverted the boys' attention back to the line. "Hey! We're almost there."

"With only seven minutes to go until show time." Louis pointed to his watch.

"Does this mean you're dropping the lawsuit?" Ray's hand flew to the side of his face as his mouth opened and his eyes widened in fake shock.

"Not necessarily." Ignoring Ray's teasing expression and remark, Louis countered with another scowl. "The candy counter is probably mobbed, which means we'll either have to get our supplies now and risk being late, or—one of us will have to volunteer to go after the movie has started."

"We've got ten minutes of coming attraction previews," Ray reminded him. "We won't starve and we won't miss the beginning of the movie. So relax, okay?"

"But I *like* the previews," Louis huffed.

The discussion ended as Louis stepped up to

the window and bought his ticket from a dour-faced woman Alex had never seen before.

As Louis rushed off to get a place in line at the refreshment counter, Ray fished a ten-dollar bill from his wallet and handed it to the cashier. "Two, please."

The woman frowned at him over the rim of her glasses. "ID first. This movie is rated PG-13."

"You're kidding, right?" Ray grinned, but the cashier wasn't joking.

"I don't make the rules," the woman snapped. "I just follow them."

Rolling his eyes and shaking his head, Ray shuffled through a bunch of cards and receipts in his wallet.

"Not you." Annoyed, the cashier pressed a button, ejecting one ticket. Then she shifted her piercing blue-eyed gaze to Alex. "Her."

Alex paled.

Planting himself firmly in front of the woman, Ray matched her stubborn stare. "She's fifteen."

"Prove it." The woman crossed her arms, indicating she was not going to back down.

"Hey!" Someone back in the line shouted. "What's the holdup?"

"Pay up or move on!" Another young voice demanded.

Sighing, Ray looked back. "Better show her your ID, Alex, or Louis will be watching *Flight of Fear* alone and we'll know everything that happens before we get a chance to come back."

"I can't," Alex rasped as she struggled to keep the embarrassed flush creeping up her neck from blossoming into a full-faced golden glow. "I left my purse at home, remember?"

Ray blinked, then slumped. "Oh, yeah."

"They all say that," the woman observed smugly.

"This is *too* good. . . ." a girl giggled.

Withering inside, Alex glanced around to see Kelly Phillips and Stacy Anderson. Kelly, who was dressed in dark brown slacks and stubby-heeled boots with a short brown tweed jacket over a cranberry shirt, quickly wiped an amused smile off her face. Stacy grinned openly. Like Kelly, she looked as if she had just stepped out of a teen magazine fashion ad. Her dark blue skirt and long vest matched, as did her beige turtleneck and over-the-knee stockings. Carrying shopping bags from The Loft, the girls had obviously just stepped out of the stylish clothing store beside the theater in time to witness Alex's humiliation.

Shoving Ray's ticket into his hand with his change, the cashier yelled, "Next!"

The boy behind Alex nudged her aside to give the stern woman in the window his money.

"I don't believe this." Furious, Ray clenched his jaw and crushed his ticket in his fist.

"These things happen." Alex shrugged, hoping to convince Ray that she wasn't as upset as he was. "You go on with Louis."

"I can't just leave you and go see a movie after that stupid woman insulted you like that!"

"It's all right, Ray. Really. You've already paid for your ticket and there's no sense wasting it. I'll see *Flight of Fear* with Robyn and Nicole some other time."

"No way. You wait right here, Alex!" Ray backed toward the entrance. "This is totally unfair and I'm gonna get the manager. And Louis! We'll see just how good a future lawyer he really is!"

"Ray! No, don't—" Before Alex could stop him, Ray disappeared through the doors.

And Kelly appeared in front of her.

"How absolutely *dreadful*, Alex." Sighing, Kelly glared at the cashier. "That woman had no right to treat you that way."

Mortified by the cashier's unexpected refusal

to sell her a ticket, the last thing Alex needed was Kelly's phony sympathy. If she could have, she would have *thought* open a hole in the floor and fallen into it. Since that wasn't an option, she was forced to face Kelly and Stacy with a demeanor of calm unconcern that was the opposite of what she really felt.

"She was just doing her job, Kelly. No big deal."

"Yes, I guess she was." Stepping back slightly, Kelly looked Alex up and down with a critical eye. "I'm not sure if it's the hat or the sweatshirt, but I know this wouldn't have happened if you had had a chance to change before you came. You really don't look your age in those bum-around-the-house clothes."

"But Alex always wears casual stuff," Stacy said with a puzzled frown.

Cheeks flaming with embarrassment, Alex froze as the telltale warmth of the golden glow tickled her skin.

"I know, Stacy," Kelly admonished gently. "But just imagine how traumatic this whole experience must be for poor Alex. I mean, how would you feel if you couldn't get in to see a PG-13 movie without an ID?"

"Oh, I don't think that would ever happen to

me," Stacy answered confidently. "I never leave the house in grubs."

"Excuse me—" Although running away would give Kelly the satisfaction of knowing she had gotten to her, Alex had no choice. She was glowing brighter than the huge Paradise Valley town Christmas tree. Shielding her face with her hand, she darted into the crowded concourse.

"Hey! Alex!" Ray's voice rang out behind her. "Where are you going? Alex!"

Stopping in the recessed entrance of Bath Boutique, Alex kept her face covered as she watched Kelly intercept Ray. She couldn't hear what Kelly was saying, but the girl apparently convinced him that he should go to the movie without her. Shoulders sagging and head hanging, Ray turned and trudged into the theater.

Staring at the display of towels and matching bathroom accessories in the window, Alex waited until her glowing reflection in the glass dimmed and her complexion returned to normal. She couldn't remember when she had been more humiliated. Being denied access to a PG-13 movie was even worse than being the unsuspecting subject of Nathan Dean's video assignment at school last year. Otherwise known as the Creeper, he had tried to flatter her with his glowing descriptions and funny footage, but he had made her the laughingstock of the whole school instead.

Worse, Alex thought as she confronted the casually comfortable look that was her fashion signature in the window glass. The knit hat, baggy sweatshirt, jeans, and high-tops did make her look younger than she was.

As difficult as it was to accept, she could not escape the annoying realization that Kelly was right.

CHAPTER 3

Upset and depressed, Alex concentrated on her feet and the roadside bike path as she pedaled home. Going to the movies to avoid writing the English essay had backfired worse than she could possibly have imagined. Having to finish the assignment that drove home her lack of career aspirations was bad enough, but now she had to cope with Kelly Phillips knowing that she had been turned away from a PG-13 film!

Still, Alex thought as she turned onto a side street through town, *school doesn't start for another ten days. Maybe Kelly will forget about the incident by then.*

And Danielle Atron might resign as the chief

executive officer of Paradise Valley Chemical to grow marigolds and knit sweaters!

Right, Alex chided herself. Hawaii would be buried by the next ice age before either one of those scenarios happened. Kelly had disliked her since she had arrived in Paradise Valley. At first, the pretty, poised girl had thought she was competition for Scott's affections. Now, even with Scott gone, Kelly's sweetly disguised attitude of disdain toward her persisted. Kelly would show no mercy.

By lunchtime a week from next Monday, Alex realized with dismal certainty, everyone in school would know what had happened to her at the mall multiplex.

"Recycle! Recycle!"

"It helps you and saves the planet, too! Recycle!"

The shouts broke into Alex's reverie. Braking, she looked down the block and saw a mob of people picketing in front of The Salty Claw, a popular seafood restaurant. Two camera crews from different local TV stations were taping the event for the evening news and a small group of curious spectators watched from the sidelines. Mounting her bike again, Alex checked for traffic, then moved into the empty street to skirt the demonstration.

"Don't throw away our future!" A familiar voice rose above the crowd's chants. "Recycle now!"

Alex turned to search the picket line as she rode slowly by and spotted Nicole walking in a large circle with the other protestors and carrying a sign that read:

The Trash You Save Today
May Save the Day Tomorrow!

Turning away, Alex started to pedal faster. Champion of the underdog and an outspoken, passionate defender of the environment, Nicole was on course toward a life dedicated to helping others and making the world a better place for everyone. Ordinarily, Alex wouldn't have dreamed of deliberately avoiding one of her best friends. But today, she really didn't want to talk to the totally committed girl, especially when Nicole was actively pursuing her goals and she had become all too aware that she didn't have any.

"Hey, Alex! Alex!" Nicole hollered. "Wait!"

But I can't just snub her, either. Stopping, Alex

braced the bike with one hand and waved as Nicole ran over.

"Where have you been, Alex? I haven't seen you since the songfest by the town tree Christmas Eve!"

"Yeah, I've been kinda busy. Family stuff because of Christmas and everything." Forcing a smile, Alex tried to hide her mood. "How was your holiday?"

"Super. My dad put together this absolutely awesome do-it-yourself protestor's kit! He meant it as a joke, of course, but—I used it to make this sign." Laughing, Nicole lowered the cardboard placard tacked to a flat wooden stake so Alex could get a better look. "I wrote that slogan, too."

"Cool." Nodding, Alex hoped her lack of enthusiasm wasn't too obvious. "Very catchy."

"Thanks." Beaming, Nicole scanned her chanting, circling associates, then gasped with surprise.

"What?" Alex asked, puzzled.

"Over there!" Nicole pointed past Alex's shoulder. "Isn't that Robyn with the KPVC news crew?"

Glancing back, Alex stared. Standing beside

Charlene Owens, one of the five o'clock news anchors on Channel Eleven, Robyn listened intently as the newscaster talked. Her red ponytail bounced as she nodded and scanned the clipboard in her hand. Then, when Ms. Owens gave her a microphone, Robyn took a deep breath, looked up, and immediately focused on her two gawking friends.

"It looks like she's working with them, doesn't it?" Nicole rested the sign on her shoulder and frowned as Robyn tugged on Charlene Owens's sleeve and pointed in their direction. "I wonder what that's all about?"

"Beats me." Shrugging, Alex wished she could just leave, but there was no way. Robyn had been talking about going into broadcast journalism for a couple of months. Now it looked as if she had decided not to wait until she finished high school and college. Microphone in hand, with a cameraman trailing behind, she was headed straight for them.

"Gosh, am I glad to see you two here." Robyn's freckled face was flushed with excitement. "I'm so nervous, I can't stand it!"

"About what?" Nicole asked, then added playfully, "Besides hanging out with the top news team in the county."

"Didn't I tell you?" Robyn blinked, then slumped when Alex and Nicole both shook their heads. "Oh, boy. It's been so hectic, I guess I forgot. Sorry."

"So tell us!" Nicole urged. "What's going on?"

Alex made a point of paying close attention as Robyn launched into a hurried explanation. She didn't want her depression to dampen Robyn's soaring spirits.

"Well, Channel Eleven decided to try including a teen viewpoint segment on their show once a week. So when Ms. Owens contacted the school for a reporter, Mrs. Broderick recommended me! I guess because I told her I was going to write about TV newscasting in my essay." Robyn's buoyant smile suddenly shifted into a worried frown.

"That is so cool!" Nicole's eyes narrowed. "So what's the problem?"

"I just got my first assignment and I'm afraid I'm going to mess it up. So please, tell me you'll help me out." Robyn's grimacing plea fell just short of begging.

"Sure. If we can. Right?" Nicole looked to Alex for support. Keeping Robyn's spirits up wasn't always easy, but they had gotten used to it over the years.

"Sure," Alex agreed with a bright smile and an energetic nod that did not betray her own misery. If nothing else, she was a good actress.

She had proven that when she had replaced Hannah Mercury as Roxanne in the school's presentation of *Cyrano de Bergerac* after the other girl had accidentally smashed her nose. In fact, Alex reflected, although she thought she could deal with the rejection and risks that went along with a dramatic arts profession, becoming an actress didn't really appeal to her. She had to spend too much time pretending she *didn't* have her unusual powers to seriously consider a career in make-believe.

"Great!" Robyn relaxed. "This will only take a few minutes. Promise."

"What will?" Nicole asked warily.

"The interview," Robyn explained. "I'm doing the teen segment of the recycling protest story and you're a teenager who's actively involved. It's perfect."

"You mean I get to say what I think on TV?" Smiling as the significance of the opportunity became apparent, Nicole lifted the sign off her shoulder so it could be seen.

"Well, since you don't really need me—" Trying to beg off gracefully, Alex swung her leg back over her bike seat. "I've got a pile of things to do at home—"

"Not so fast, Alex!" Robyn gently grabbed her arm. "I want your perspective as a concerned teenaged citizen."

"But I—" The objection died in Alex's throat. Robyn was always there when she needed help, like last Christmas when she had talked her father into donating the large, detached garage near his funeral home so the elderly elf-squad had a place to work fixing toys for needy kids. If Robyn wanted her opinion for a TV news segment, she couldn't refuse. Especially since Charlene Owens was standing nearby, watching every move Robyn made with a kind but critical eye. "Okay. I'm in."

"Cool. Here goes nothing!" Motioning the cameraman closer, Robyn turned to face him, then smoothed her skirt and straightened her tailored jacket. Nodding to start the camera rolling, she delivered her opening lines without a hint of nervousness.

"Good evening. I'm Robyn Russo reporting from the The Salty Claw in Paradise Valley, where a large group of ecologically concerned citizens are protesting the restaurant's refusal to institute a recycling policy. With me are two local high school students, Alex Mack—"

Alex smiled tightly as Robyn gestured toward her, then paled when she realized that she would be seen on television wearing a knit hat, sweatshirt, and jeans! She could have taken off the hat if she had thought of it sooner, but the camera had already committed her to tape and it was too late. The only thing working in her favor was that not a lot of kids watched the evening news and Kelly hadn't had a chance to pass the word about her public ridicule at the theater—yet.

"So tell me, Nicole. Why are you demonstrating today?" Robyn held the mike up to Nicole's mouth as if she had been conducting TV interviews all her life.

"I'm here because I believe that recycling is essential to the planet's ecological welfare in the future." Nicole spoke with a steady voice and firm resolve. "It doesn't make sense to throw away containers that can be processed and used again."

Alex noticed that Nicole's fellow protestors had stopped walking to watch. Cued by her key phrase, they all began to yell.

"Use it again! Use it again!"

Charlene Owens silenced them with a raised hand and a sharp look, then motioned the cameraman to keep taping.

Completely unflustered by the crowd's interruption, Robyn continued. "But the The Salty Claw doesn't recycle its refuse. Is that correct?"

"Yes, it is. And that doesn't make sense, either, because recycling is so easy!" Nicole became more animated as she warmed up. "They don't have to take the time or the trouble to haul their usable trash anywhere. They just have to separate it into bins provided by the city and then the city picks it up!"

Alex was impressed with how well both her friends were handling themselves, and judging by her smiling expression, Charlene Owens was extremely pleased, too.

"And what brings you here, Alex?"

Focused on Nicole and Ms. Owens, Alex was caught completely off guard when Robyn addressed her.

"Uh, I was just passing by." Flinching slightly when Robyn hesitated for a split second, Alex realized the fledgling reporter had been expecting an answer that was pertinent to the subject of recycling. Embarrassed again, she desperately tried to stay calm when a foreboding warmth tickled the back of her neck. Danielle Atron *did* watch the evening news, and she would be very interested in a girl who suddenly developed an inexplicable case of golden glow.

Deftly covering her momentary surprise, Robyn forged ahead. "What are your thoughts on the mandatory recycling ordinance the Paradise Valley City Council is considering?"

"I didn't know—" Alex stopped herself and valiantly tried to answer intelligently, but it was difficult to think clearly when she was concentrating most of her energies on *not* glowing. "I think it would be a great idea to force everyone to save their trash."

Although her thought was appropriate, Alex knew her choice of words was not. Ms. Owens apparently agreed, because she immediately signaled Robyn to wrap it up. That was fine with Alex. Embarrassed, nervous, and on the verge of a luminous blush that she didn't want captured on tape, she was more than ready to leave.

"Do you recycle at home?"

"Yes, we do," Alex answered flatly.

Facing the camera again, Robyn closed like a

pro. "And that's the *Teen Take* in Paradise Valley tonight. This is Robyn Russo for Channel Eleven News."

Everyone remained quiet as the cameraman rolled tape for several more seconds. The instant he shut down, the demonstrators rushed Nicole to congratulate her with cheers and applause.

"Way to go, Nicole!"

"That was a terrific plug!"

"Maybe now the city will act on that recycling ordinance!"

Grinning from ear to ear, Nicole soaked up the praise with speechless satisfaction.

Easing through the crush, Charlene Owens took the microphone back from Robyn and shook her hand. "That was superb, Robyn! Nicole was an excellent interview subject and I think you've got a great piece to air tonight."

"Tonight?" Robyn squealed. "Really?"

Charlene nodded. "Absolutely. It's a perfect companion bit for the lead story. But we've got to get back to the studio and start editing if it's going to be ready on time."

No one noticed as Alex slipped out of the

crowd to retrieve her bike, and she pedaled off to a chorus of renewed chanting.

"Use it again! Use it again! O-ver and o-ver! Use it again—"

Riding through town, Alex was uncomfortably aware of the glittering gold and silver Christmas decorations attached to streetlamps and strung overhead. The bright, sparkling foils and lights were a stark contrast to her dreary mood and self-image. Although she was honestly happy for Robyn and Nicole, the interview had been horrible for her. Aside from almost exposing herself as the GC-161 kid with her blazing, golden glow, she had sounded like a brainless idiot! She wouldn't blame Robyn and Charlene Owens if they left her lying on the cutting-room floor when the tape was edited. Except for the disquieting knowledge that her poor performance and lack of self-confidence would prompt their decision, being omitted from Robyn's teen segment would actually be a blessing.

Fuming with frustration, Alex telekinetically pushed a low-hanging tree branch aside and pedaled faster.

Just because I have finally accepted the fact that there is nothing extraordinary about me doesn't mean I want to advertise it on TV!

Struck by a zapper from her finger, a soda can clattered out of the bike's path.

Alex pumped with a fury that increased in direct proportion to her mounting anguish. Everyone she knew, her family and close friends, had some distinctive personality trait and talent that defined them. All she had was her powers, which were a secret and didn't count. Before she had been genetically altered by the experimental compound GC-161, she had gone through a period of feeling totally ordinary and dull. That hadn't bothered her for a long time, but time did not erase the truth. Without the powers, she was still just an ordinary kid.

That had not been easy to accept when she was entering junior high. It was even harder to accept now that she was in high school and adulthood loomed.

Coming to a T intersection, Alex slammed on the brakes and stared at a sign in the front window of a quaint neighborhood restaurant straight ahead.

Make Your New Year's Resolutions Here!
Only $49.95 per Couple!

The new year was only a week away. What better time to evaluate who she was and who she wanted to be?

A determined resolve suddenly arrowed through the overwhelming despair.

She didn't have to accept being plain old Alex Mack.

She could change.

CHAPTER 4

"Mom!" Alex ran all the way upstairs before she remembered that her mother was at a planning meeting for the New Year's Eve gala with the mayor's wife.

Having resolved to seriously begin exploring realistic career opportunities, Alex wanted to get off to a solid start with some sound and educated advice. Her mom was an excellent source. During her years in public relations, Mrs. Mack had dealt with all kinds of people in dozens of different occupations. With her help, Alex was hoping to discover some obscure but exciting profession that not only appealed to her, but suited her own as-yet-undiscovered aptitudes.

But that would have to wait until the meeting was over at six-thirty.

Disappointed, Alex trudged into the bedroom that was all hers now—most of the time. Absently tossing her hat on Annie's perfectly made bed, she stopped short. All of Annie's side was in immaculate order, the unmistakable evidence that her older sister was back in temporary residence. Alex had gotten into the habit of using her sister's bed as a convenient dumping ground over the past few months. The day Annie had come home from school for the holidays, it had taken Alex all morning to put away the pile of stuff that had landed there since September.

But that wouldn't happen again, she decided. Getting organized was essential to success, regardless of what she finally chose to do with her life.

Picking up the knit cap, Alex dropped it in a drawer and shoved the drawer closed.

The hats had to go, too. She had started collecting and wearing them as a means of self-expression when she was in elementary school, but they were totally unsuitable for the more mature Alex Mack that was about to emerge.

In fact, Alex realized, catching a glimpse of herself in the mirror, everything about her appearance was all wrong. How could she expect anyone to take her seriously when she looked like a kid? If she wanted to be treated like a responsible adult, she had to dress and act like one.

And there was no time like the present to start making the necessary changes. Grabbing a robe, Alex headed for the shower.

An hour later, as she finished securing her hair in a ponytail high on her head, Alex stepped back to study the results. With her hair pulled severely back off her face, the tailored white blouse and dark brown slacks her aunt had given her for Christmas, worn with stockings and black flats, created the more mature look she had wanted to achieve. Small pearl earrings and a dark brown leather shoulder bag she had borrowed from her mother's closet completed the outward image of businesslike intent and poise.

She hardly looked like herself at all.

A twinge of misgiving flashed through Alex's mind as the dramatic effect of her new wardrobe sank in. This wasn't the first time she had changed her appearance because she was tired of being just another ordinary face in the crowd. Enamored of a new girl's rebellious image, she had totally freaked out and adopted Lindsay's flamboyant, far-out style. But she had completely misjudged Lindsay's character based on the girl's weird clothes, outrageous hair, body piercings, and tattoos, and she had almost lost her as a friend because of it.

Frowning thoughtfully, Alex pondered her sedate reflection and concluded that this change wasn't even remotely similar. This time, she wasn't trying to look or be like someone else. She was merely enhancing herself.

Switching her things from a crocheted carryall into her mother's leather bag, Alex also resolved not to make the same mistake about her future career as she had with cheerleading. She had gone out for the team because cheerleaders were respected and popular—not because she really enjoyed cheerleading. But she hadn't known just how much work and dedication went into being on the squad. The time devoted to practice, fundraising projects, and attending all the actual sporting events was enormous, which wouldn't have been a problem if she had loved the position and prestige as much as did Kelly Phillips. Disillusioned and convinced that she probably would have been voted in as the alternate if she hadn't telekinetically trapped Kelly's pompoms in the rafters at the tryouts, Alex had gladly stepped aside.

But she *had* learned a valuable lesson. She had to really *like* whatever career she chose or she'd be miserable.

Slipping the bag strap onto her shoulder, Alex looked out the window. Her whole life depended on the choices she made in the next few years. Maybe even in the next few months. Every move and decision from now on would cement a stone in the foundation of her future. And her future would only be as solid as the foundation. She could no longer afford to do anything on impulse or whim, because the repercussions might have potentially harmful effects years down the road.

Alex needed a plan and her mother to help her formulate one. However, her mom was so busy with the preparations for the New Year's Eve gala, she might be hard to pin down during the next few days. Although Alex didn't expect to settle on a career overnight, she at least wanted to write a relatively honest career essay. If she timed it just right, she might be able to intercept her mom when she left City Hall after the planning meeting. Then they could talk on the ride home.

Turning to leave, Alex telekinetically reached to pick up the towel she had dropped on the floor, then thought better of it. It was time she took Annie's advice seriously, too, and stopped using her powers frivolously. One false step and Danielle Atron would put an abrupt end to all her plans. Picking up the towel by hand, she dropped it in the bathroom hamper on her way downstairs.

Too motivated and excited to pass the time sitting around the house, Alex headed back to the mall on foot. Growing up with two scientists, she knew that all innovative scientific developments were subjected to field experiments to prove whether they worked. The movie would be letting out shortly after she arrived and she wanted to test the impact of her altered appearance on Ray and Louis. Especially Louis. As Ray had pointed out earlier, the wanna-be lawyer was totally honest to the point of being blunt. She could count on Louis Driscoll to say exactly what he thought.

Alex walked through the outer doors and into the main concourse at five-twenty, ten minutes before the film ended. The mall was even more crowded than it had been earlier, probably because people who had just gotten off work were making their exchanges and returns on their way home. Bracing herself to be crushed and jostled in the mass of weary, anxious shoppers, she eased into the pedestrian traffic and headed toward the theater. She was pleasantly surprised when several harried adults moved aside to let her pass or excused themselves after accidently bumping into her. It was immediately apparent that they didn't perceive her as an annoying kid who was just hanging out, which sent her morale soaring sky high.

When she reached the theater, Alex noticed that the line for the six o'clock showing of *Flight of Fear* was a lot shorter, no doubt because the admission price was higher than for the matinee. The same woman was still seated behind the ticket window, too. Wondering if the cranky cashier would ask to see her ID now, Alex got into line. Ray and Louis wouldn't be coming out for another five minutes and she couldn't resist the additional chance to test her new look.

"How many?" The woman asked sharply.

Holding out a ten-dollar bill, Alex hesitated in anticipation of the dreaded ID question.

"Do you want a ticket or not?" The cashier snapped, looking Alex directly in the eye.

"No, thank you." Smiling, Alex snatched back

her money and stepped aside as the woman rolled her eyes and impatiently waved the next customer up to the window.

Pass!

Elated with the results of her impromptu experiment, Alex almost laughed aloud. Restraining herself, she stood ten feet in front of the exit and concentrated on maintaining an expression of detached unconcern as a mob of mostly teens filed out. When Ray and Louis finally appeared, she made a point of looking in their direction without actually looking at them.

"No way, Ray," Louis exclaimed. "That was ten times better than *Warlords of Mars*."

"Come off it, Louis. The special effects were better, but the plot had more holes in it than a Chinese checkers game board!"

"Maybe, but who cares?"

Alex tensed as Louis and Ray passed a mere four feet away from her without a glance. Of course, they weren't expecting to see her waiting and the friendly argument had their full attention.

"I mean, so what if the captain jumped to a few conclusions and made decisions that almost got everyone killed and the ship blown up?

Somebody had to do something dumb or there wouldn't have been any action!"

"Wrong." Ray rolled his eyes. "First of all, nobody that stupid would ever get command of such an important mission in real life."

Louis raised a skeptical eyebrow. "Don't you ever watch the evening news?"

"Maybe it's a good thing I missed it," Alex said.

Ray paused and looked up with a puzzled frown.

"That sounded like Alex." As Louis's gaze swept the crowd, it flicked right by her, then suddenly flicked back. "There she is!" He blinked. "I think."

"Alex?" Ray followed as Louis shouldered his way over. "What did you do? You look so— different."

"Different and totally awesome!" Louis nodded with an approving grin.

Alex just smiled. Her field test had been one hundred percent successful.

CHAPTER 5

The rush of elation Alex felt subsided almost instantly when she noticed Ray's uncertain frown. "What's the matter?"

"Nothing. It's just that—" Shrugging, Ray hesitated. "Never mind."

"So what are you doing here, Alex?" Louis asked.

"Yeah." Ray jumped in before she could answer. "If you came back to see *Flight of Fear* by yourself because you're worried that we're gonna tell you about it and spoil it—don't. It's not that good."

"That depends on whether you think action is more important than a perfect plot." Louis rolled his eyes and shifted his attention from Ray to Alex. "Personally, I liked it. Enough to go see it again, if you want company."

"It's a waste of time, Alex," Ray persisted. "Come with us to the Half-Life Café instead."

"*After* we drop a few quarters at the Palisade Arcade," Louis added. "Today may be the day I finally top the high score on Planetary Conquest."

"Thanks, but I can't," Alex said apologetically. Although she appreciated the invitation, she had more important things to do than play arcade video games. "I've got to get to City Hall before my mom finishes her meeting with the mayor's wife."

"The mayor's wife?" Ray started, then grinned. "Oh, well, that explains it."

"Explains what?" Alex asked, puzzled.

"The strictly business duds." Louis grimaced slightly. "They lack that distinctive Alex Mack signature of mismatched casual we've all come to know and love."

"Yeah," Ray agreed. "Now you look just like everyone else. Great, but—there's no individual flair."

Bristling slightly, Alex quickly calmed herself. They hadn't meant to insult her. They were probably just overreacting because her change in style was so sudden and unexpected.

"I'd better get moving or I'll be late. I'll catch you later." Nodding a reserved farewell, Alex turned and walked briskly toward the exit. She hoped Ray and Louis didn't interpret her abrupt departure as a snub. She just didn't want them to see how much their criticism hurt.

Passing an electronics store displaying television sets in the window, Alex paused with a startled gasp. Every screen was showing Robyn interviewing Nicole. Charlene Owens and Robyn must have worked nonstop to get the piece edited in time for the evening news. Grateful that Louis and Ray weren't with her, she stepped inside to watch the rest of the Channel Eleven teen segment.

"*. . . and then the city picks it up!*"

Alex tensed as the camera swung away from Nicole to Robyn, hoping that the interview ended there. No such luck. The picture switched to show her in her knit cap and sweatshirt with a pained expression as she tried not to glow. Robyn's question was asked in a voiceover. As Alex had suspected, most of her part had been edited out.

"*Do you re-cycle at home?*"

"Yes, we do."

"And that's the Teen Take—"

Alex suddenly became aware of the salesman standing behind her.

"Does anyone really care what some kid thinks?" The man shook his head

"Kids care," Alex said coolly.

"I suppose." The man shrugged, then smiled. "Can I help you?"

"Not today. Thank you." As she hurried out and toward the mall exit, Alex actually felt better. The salesman hadn't realized she was the same "dumb kid" he had seen on the broadcast, and her shaken confidence in her new look was restored. Eventually, Ray and her other friends would accept it, too. Inside she was still Alex Mack. Only the packaging had been changed and she was convinced that change was for the better.

Taking the bus to save time, Alex arrived at City Hall at six-fifteen. The building was officially closed, but the security guard at the front door patiently listened to her explanation. If her resolve about adopting a more adult attitude and appearance hadn't already been firmly entrenched, his unquestioning acceptance of her presence would have cinched it.

"Mrs. Lincoln and your mother are in room one-twelve." The guard pointed and gave her directions. "Down that hall on your left."

"Thank you." Smiling warmly, Alex entered the deserted building and found the room with no trouble. She had intended to wait outside the room, but the door was open.

"Hi!" Looking up from a table strewn with papers, Mrs. Mack smiled with delighted surprise. "What are you doing here?"

Alex was aware of her mother's quick and questioning glance regarding her wardrobe. However, although her mom was obviously puzzled, she didn't say a word about the dramatic change, saving Alex from having to explain in front of the mayor's wife. "I thought we could ride home together. I didn't mean to interrupt."

"Don't worry about it. Come on in."

"Is this your daughter?" Valerie Lincoln, a trim, impeccably dressed woman of fifty with short, softly curled dark hair that was just starting to turn gray, stood up and extended her hand. "How do you like MIT, Annie?"

Alex suppressed a surprised gasp as her mother quickly corrected the woman's mistaken assumption.

"This is my younger daughter, Al—"

"Alexandra. How do you do, Mrs. Lincoln?" Shaking the offered hand, Alex smiled warmly and ignored her mother's startled glance. Somehow, her full given name seemed more appropriate for an introduction to the mayor's wife. And once she had said it, it sounded right, too.

"I'm just fine—considering." Sighing, Mrs. Lincoln sat back down and stared at the piles of papers. "So many people are out of town for the holidays, we're desperately short of volunteers to help with the teen gala."

"That's a major understatement." Matching Mrs. Lincoln's sigh, Mrs. Mack pushed a stray lock of blond hair back over her ear.

"Is there something I can do to help?" Alex asked.

Mrs. Lincoln and Mrs. Mack both looked up sharply.

"We need someone to distribute and hang posters around town," Mrs. Lincoln said hopefully.

"I can do that," Alex said with instant enthusiasm.

"It's a big job," Mrs. Mack cautioned. Even so, her expression brightened at Alex's offer to lend a hand.

"Not a problem. I'm sure I can get some of

my friends to pitch in." Although Alex had volunteered to help on impulse, suddenly the pros-
pect of getting directly involved in the major
teen social event was exactly what she wanted
to do. Working with Mrs. Lincoln and her
mother would certainly hone her dismal organi-
zational skills, and she might even find she had
an interest in civic service or a flair for public
relations like her mom.

Or advertising, Alex thought as Mrs. Lincoln
held up one of the printed posters.

"What do you think, Alexandra?" Mrs. Lincoln asked.

Alex paused, appearing to study the poster
when she was actually trying to figure out how
to voice an honest opinion without being too
harsh. Measuring roughly fourteen by twenty
inches, the poster looked like any generic ad for
New Year's Eve. The text naming the event and
giving the date, time, and place was printed in
bold black block letters and the graphics depicted noisemakers, party hats, confetti, and bub-
bles coming out of a champagne bottle with the
word "soda" printed on the label. It wouldn't
attract a teenager to a top-forty CD giveaway at
Hot Hits in the mall.

"Did you design this, Mom?"

Smiling tightly, Mrs. Mack shook her head. "No. We're working on a limited budget and had to settle for graphics the printer had in stock."

"Well, it's a little bland, but it gives all the necessary information." Noting the disappointed look on Mrs. Lincoln's face, Alex risked making a suggestion. "But if you don't mind, we might be able to snaz it up with some colors. Circling or underlining the important words and adding an exclamation point or two—that kind of thing."

"That's a great idea!" Mrs. Mack beamed.

Mrs. Lincoln pointed to a cardboard box full of posters. "We've got plenty, Alexandra. Change them if you want and hang them wherever you think they'll do the most good. The job's yours. And thanks."

"Glad to do it." Alex paused thoughtfully. "You know, I might be able to get a free plug on Channel Eleven."

"A *free* TV spot? Like mother, like daughter," Mrs. Lincoln observed. "You didn't tell me your talent for getting things done ran in the family, Barbara."

"Uh, well—we Macks are just full of sur-

prises." Mrs. Mack looked at Alex in uncon-
cealed astonishment. "TV?"

"Robyn's doing a weekly spot from the teenage point of view," Alex explained.

"Excellent!" Mrs. Lincoln scratched something
off a list in front of her. "So now that poster
distribution is covered, we've got one less problem to deal with."

"Shouldn't the name of the band be on the
posters?" Alex asked.

"It should." Mrs. Mack sat down wearily. "But
it's a good thing we *didn't* name the band. The
group we booked got a better offer and canceled
before we signed the contract."

Mrs. Lincoln sighed. "At this late date, we'll
be hard-pressed to find anyone else."

"But we're working on it," Mrs. Mack assured
her. "At least we've got the Community Center
set."

"And the refreshments and maybe the decorations," Mrs. Lincoln added.

"Maybe?" Alex asked.

"I'm afraid the Paradise Valley Women's Auxiliary's idea of decorations is bud vases and
place cards on tables." Mrs. Mack laughed when
Alex winced. "Don't worry. I'm working on that,
too. The band's a bigger problem."

"A good DJ with CDs would work just as well," Alex suggested.

Mrs. Mack nodded. "I'll look into that, Alex. Thanks."

"I don't mean to push," Mrs. Lincoln interjected, "but when do you think you can get started posting the posters?"

"Well, if you've got a phone I can use, I'm pretty sure I can have a group organized and ready to go in the morning."

Mrs. Lincoln waved toward the door. "My husband's office is across the hall."

Left alone in the mayor's office, Alex sat behind the huge polished mahogany desk with a distinct sense of awe. She had gone from PG-13 movie reject to being accepted as a member of an adult planning committee in a matter of hours. And all because she had made a decision and acted on it. Looking around at the shelves of books lining the walls, the signed photographs of various important people, and the state-of-the-art computer system, leather chairs and multiple-line phone, she realized that at that rate of progress, she could end up *being* the mayor of Paradise Valley someday. All she had to do was decide what she wanted and go for it.

And deliver.

Picking up the phone, Alex dialed Robyn's house. Mrs. Russo answered, complimented her brief appearance on the evening news, then explained that Robyn was meeting Nicole at the Half-Life Café after she left the KPVC studio. Since Ray and Louis were going to the popular teen hangout, too, there was no problem getting everyone together. She just hoped convincing them to help would be as easy.

"Are you going to be leaving soon, Mom?" Alex asked when she got back to room 112.

"No, not for a while. Valerie has something unrelated to the gala she wants to discuss."

"I'm taking full advantage of your mother's public relations expertise while I've got the chance." Mrs. Lincoln winked.

"Do you need a ride, Alex?"

"No. I can walk to the Half-Life to meet my friends, but could you bring the box of posters home in the car?"

"Sure." As Alex turned to leave, Mrs. Mack called after her. "We can talk over pizza when I get there, okay?"

"You're on. See ya then!" Slinging her mother's bag over her shoulder, Alex dashed out the door.

As usual on a Friday night, the Half-Life was

full of kids drinking sodas, sharing fries, laughing, and talking. Nicole, Robyn, Louis, and Ray were sitting in the last booth. Kelly, Stacy Anderson, and Craig Hawkins, a good-looking varsity football player who had just transferred to Paradise High from upstate, were seated at a booth near the door.

"Who is *that?*" Craig asked Kelly, his gaze fixed on Alex as she started down the aisle.

"Who?" Kelly looked up and shrugged. "I don't know—Alex?"

Alex cast a casual glance at Kelly as she passed by. "Hello, Kelly."

Kelly just stared.

Walking on without pause, Alex smiled when she heard Craig press Kelly for more information.

"Alex who? Does she go to our school?"

On a roll and loving it, Alex was bubbling over with eagerness when she reached her friends. "Hi! Got room for one more?"

"There's always room for you, Alex." Forcing Louis against the wall, Ray scooted over to make space on the end of the seat.

"Thanks." Sitting down, Alex immediately launched into her pitch for help to modify and hang the posters. "If you could all come to my house in the morning, we can have the posters changed and distributed by late afternoon."

"I'd have to miss the afternoon picketing session outside The Salty Claw, but—" Nicole shrugged. "TAR has plenty of volunteers and you don't. I'll be there."

"Tar?" Louis grimaced. "What's that?"

"The Advocates for Recycling," Nicole explained patiently.

Robyn sighed. "I don't have a clue what to do for next week's *Teen Take* spot, so I might as well beg storekeepers to let me put posters in their windows. And hope they agree—which they may not."

"I can think of better ways to spend a whole day of Christmas vacation," Louis muttered.

"Me, too." Ray elbowed him slightly and grinned. "But we're still going to help Alex, aren't we?"

"Guess so. In self-defense." Rubbing his arm, Louis scowled. "How did your mom and the mayor's wife stick you with running posters around town, anyway, Alex?"

"They didn't 'stick' me with it. I volunteered."

"Why?" Louis looked genuinely perplexed.

"Mostly because I want to make sure the New Year's Eve gala is as much fun for us as it can be. Like I said, the posters need a little tweaking, and on top of that, the Women's Auxiliary wants to use some totally dorky decorations, and the band canceled. I might be able to use my influence to make sure they hire somebody really cool."

"So when did you turn into a mover and shaker?" Robyn asked curiously.

"Since she changed her basic look, I imagine." Nicole grinned mischievously. "About four-thirty this afternoon, right, Alex?"

"That much is obvious." Ray's jovial expression shifted to one of concern. "The real question is, why?"

"Because I'm not twelve anymore and I just decided to stop dressing and acting like I was. It's that simple." Alex's statement was met with bewildered frowns around the table.

"Oh! You made a New Year's resolution!" Louis brightened. "Don't worry, Ray. Nobody *ever* keeps their resolutions. She'll be her old self before the new year even starts."

"There's more to it than that," Alex countered flatly. "I can't avoid growing up. None of us can."

"What's that supposed to mean?" Nicole wasn't upset. She honestly didn't understand.

Alex sighed. "For me, it means that I have to start thinking seriously about my future. What I want to do. That sort of thing. I've just been going from day to day like I haven't got a care in the world."

"You don't," Louis quipped. "Except for homework and getting from one class to another before the bell rings."

"I think she's got a point," Ray said. "The truth is, I don't have a clue what I really want to do with my life, either. That's probably why I'm always changing my mind."

"You're always changing your mind about a lot of things, Ray," Louis said. "One of these days maybe you'll make a decision and stick to it."

"And maybe you'll figure out how to say what you mean without being so painfully blunt, Louis." Nicole eyed him coldly.

"Actually, that wouldn't be a bad New Year's resolution for me." Ray nodded thoughtfully for a moment, then took a deep breath. "From now on, if I make a decision, I'm going to follow through."

"You can do it, Ray." Alex smiled, delighted that she was having such a positive effect.

"I give it seventy-two hours," Louis said. "Tops."

"Take a hint, Louis." Robyn looked at him askance. "It wouldn't hurt you to try being less outspoken and more tactful."

"Forty-eight hours." Nicole grinned. "Tops."

Shifting uncomfortably, Louis glared back. "You two aren't exactly pillars of perfection, you know? There's two sides to every story, Nicole. And maybe bad things happen to you, Robyn, because that's what you expect."

"Good thing you didn't make your resolution, yet, Louis," Ray teased. "You wouldn't have lasted more than thirty seconds."

"True." Nicole sighed. "But he's right. Maybe I should consider all the different perspectives and angles of a situation before I take a stand."

"Is that your resolution?" Alex asked.

"Sure. Why not?"

Robyn's thoughtful frown deepened. "I've always heard that positive thinking works. Guess I'll give it a shot."

Ray gave her a thumbs-up, then everyone turned to stare at Louis.

"All right! I won't be so brutally honest. Does that make everyone happy?"

"Yes!" They chorused.

"Maybe we should give ourselves a realistic time frame for sticking to our resolutions, though," Nicole suggested. "Kind of like a dry run to see how things go."

"How about until midnight New Year's Eve?" Alex glanced around the table.

Louis looked at his watch. "That's only five days, four hours, and fifteen minutes. I can do that."

Everyone else nodded.

"No matter what," Ray emphasized.

"Absolutely." Nicole heaved a resigned sigh.

Alex sat back with a profound sense of satisfaction. Just by setting an example, she had prompted her friends into trying changes that would make them better people, if they succeeded.

Radical changes.

By definition, that was a lot more significant than the ordinary resolutions most people made.

It would be a New Year's revolution.

CHAPTER 6

Alex burst through the front door and hurried into the kitchen just as her mother set a pizza box on the counter.

"You're just in time!" Turning abruptly, Mrs. Mack snagged the shoulder strap of her bag on the cardboard corner of the box and dragged it. "What—?"

Without thinking, Alex telekinetically held and leveled the box, which was extended more than halfway off the counter.

Reacting instantly as she glanced back, Mrs. Mack shoved the box to safety and dropped her purse. "That was close. And clumsy," she added with a sheepish grin. "That's the second time today I almost dumped something all over the kitchen floor."

"Almost doesn't count." Relieved that her mother had been too startled to notice the box's impossible balancing act, Alex slipped her own bag off her shoulder, picked up her mom's, and set both on the table. She also experienced a fleeting twinge of guilt about the telekinetic assist. However, it was easy to convince herself she hadn't broken her resolution already. Saving the pizza could hardly be considered a frivolous use of her powers. She was famished. "Is one pizza enough for all of us?"

"It's just you and me tonight." Removing two plates from the cupboard and grabbing two forks from the drawer, Mrs. Mack went to the table. "Annie's eating out with Christine, and your father decided to work late. Get the box, will you?"

"Sure." Shifting the pizza to the table, Alex asked. "Want anything to drink?"

"Just water." Sitting down, Mrs. Mack pulled several napkins out of the holder and divided them between the two places she had set. "Actually, I'm glad we've got this time alone."

"Me, too." Falling wearily into a chair, Alex

caught her mother staring at her. "What? Is there dirt on my face or something?"

"No." Laughing, Mrs. Mack opened the pizza and slid a steaming slice covered with tomato sauce, cheese, and pepperoni onto Alex's plate. "You look fabulous, but you didn't have to change clothes just because you knew I was with Valerie Lincoln."

"I didn't." Blowing on the hot pie, Alex took a small bite. "This outfit is *exactly* the kind of thing I want to wear from now on."

"Oh. How come?" Mrs. Mack asked, puzzled.

"I'm fifteen going on sixteen."

"Of course." Nodding, Mrs. Mack helped herself to pizza, then discreetly changed the subject. "The poster box is still in the car, but I remembered it. A wonder considering everything I've got on my mind right now."

"Well, you can stop worrying about the posters, Mom. I've got some markers and I think I'll sacrifice a few to a little artistic experimentation tonight. If I figure out *how* to change them before everyone gets here tomorrow morning, we'll save a lot of time."

"Offering to handle that job was a huge help. And your ideas were inspired. I was so proud of you this evening, Alex." Mrs. Mack paused uncertainly. "Or do you really want to be called Alexandra?"

"No." Alex shrugged, feeling a bit foolish. "Only in special cases. Like the mayor's wife."

"Speaking of the mayor's wife—Valerie is not easily impressed, but she thought you were one of the most charming and intelligent young women she's ever met."

"She said that!" Overwhelmed, Alex couldn't help laughing. "Cool!"

"Totally."

A delicious few moments of silence followed as they both devoured their first slice. Alex wasn't sure which was more savory: the pizza, Mrs. Lincoln's compliment, or her mother's delighted pride.

"Now, what did you want to talk to me about? I'm ashamed to say that I was so rushed and frantic this afternoon, I've forgotten." Taking a second slice of pizza, Mrs. Mack gave Alex her full attention.

"Actually, I was curious about how you chose public relations as a career."

"Well, let's see. I'm not exactly sure." Putting down her pizza, Mrs. Mack folded her arms. "I was always on the organizing committees for student events in high school. Dances, bake sales, the usual stuff.''

Alex listened intently as she chewed.

''And because I seemed to have a knack for getting everyone to work together and making sure everything got done, I always ended up being the one who coordinated the different sub-committees and reported to the faculty. Plus I had a flair for advertising—what would work and what wouldn't. Like what you had to say about those awful posters today.''

''Really?'' Alex hesitated, then decided to ask the question that suddenly popped into her mind. She could count on her mother to be honest. ''Do you think I might have the same kind of knack? For public relations work? I mean, I want to be really good at whatever career I go into.''

Mrs. Mack's eyes widened. ''And you're thinking about public relations?''

''It's crossed my mind.'' So far, her brief brush with the PR field had been a success. It couldn't hurt to investigate the possiblities. And judging by the smile on her mother's face, the idea appealed to her, too.

''Then, yes, Alex,'' Mrs. Mack said seriously. ''I think you do have a knack. And I'm not just saying that because I'm happy you may want to follow in my footsteps, either. Don't forget how you got your friends and all those senior citizens pulling together to fix toys for needy children at Christmas last year. That was a major undertaking and you did it. Against great odds, too."

"It was fun."

"Right. It was," her mother said pointedly.

Alex sat back with a huge smile of her own. She wanted to be good at what she did, and *like* it. The truth was that she hadn't faked her enthusiasm about distributing the posters for her mother's and Mrs. Lincoln's benefit. She was really looking foward to tackling the job and getting it done right. Her career essay for English was quickly taking shape in her mind, too.

"Well, I'm sure helping you with the New Year's Eve gala will be fun, too, Mom. And educational."

"To be honest, I'm thrilled we're going to be working together on this project." Mrs. Mack leaned forward eagerly. "Your teenaged perspective and input are really sound, and together we just might pull off a dynamite party for the town teens in spite of the limited budget."

"Guaranteed." Alex raised her hand for a high

five and grinned as her mother slapped her palm.

"You wouldn't happen to have any bright ideas about how to decorate on little or no money, would you?" Mrs. Mack asked as she picked up her pizza and bit off the pointy end.

"No, but I'll certainly give it some thought." Finishing off her second piece, Alex sighed. "So what other PR problem did Mrs. Lincoln want to talk about? Or is that confidential?"

"Not at all. In fact, if it works out, it might be extremely beneficial for the entire community. Walter Dobbs, the founder and CEO of Dobbs Manufacturing, is considering building his new plant here." Lapsing into pensive thought, Mrs. Mack stared into space as she chewed.

"Gosh! That would break Danielle Atron's hold on Paradise Valley, wouldn't it? I mean, if almost everyone wasn't so dependent on Paradise Valley Chemical because there was someplace else to work, she couldn't control everything the way she does."

And if Danielle is busy trying to keep her little empire from falling apart, Alex thought hopefully, *she might not have the time and means to look for the GC-161 kid anymore!*

"Theoretically, that's true, Alex. Having a second major industry in Paradise Valley would mean more jobs and would certainly give the town an economic boost. On the surface, it sure sounds good, but—''

''But what?'' Alex prodded.

''Well, there could be harmful effects no one's considered yet. If there are, I'll find out. I told Valerie I'd donate my time and PR expertise to help convince Walter Dobbs that Paradise Valley is perfect for his needs. He's arriving tomorrow with his daughter, Kimberly.''

Alex frowned. ''You're going to try and convince him to move his plant here and look for reasons why he shouldn't at the same time? I don't get it.''

Mrs. Mack tried to explain. ''The best way to analyze the situation, such as the effects of another plant on the town and Mr. Dobbs's motivations and intentions, is to be in the middle of everything that's going on. And the best way to do that is to work directly with Mr. Dobbs. I'll be representing Paradise Valley—not him. If there's a good reason not to allow Dobbs Manufacturing to build here, it's my job to give that information to my client—the town.''

Alex sighed. ''This PR stuff is a lot more complicated than I thought.''

"Just stick with me, kid." Mrs. Mack spoke in a playful rasping voice and cuffed Alex gently on the arm. "I'll show ya the ropes."

Grinning, Alex gave her Mom a thumbs-up. "And if there's anything I can do to help out with the Dobbs Manufacturing thing, just let me know, okay?"

"Okay. But I think we'll probably be keeping you pretty busy working on the gala. Especially now that I'm going to be spending a lot of time with Walter Dobbs. He's arriving tomorrow afternoon to take a look around."

"Speaking of the gala—" Rising, Alex took her plate and glass to the sink, rinsed them off, and put them in the dishwasher. "I'd better get going on those posters."

"I hope there's some of that pizza left for me!" Looking tired and frazzled, Mr. Mack walked into the kitchen from the living room and headed straight for the table. "I'm really hungry."

"Hi, Dad! There's more than half of it left."

"That might be enough." Taking the seat Alex had just left, Mr. Mack pulled the box toward him.

"I thought you were going to get a sandwich out of the cafeteria machines, George." Mrs.

Mack gave him her stern "you-ought-to-take-care-of-yourself-better" look.

"I did. I even ate it. Stale bread, hard cheese, wilted lettuce, and all." Mr. Mack shuddered and made a face as Alex put a plate, fork, and glass of milk in front of him. "Thanks, Alex." Then he did a double take.

"You're welcome. I've gotta go."

"Have you got a date?" Mr. Mack tried not to look worried. "You're all dressed up."

Alex rolled her eyes. "No, I don't have a date."

"She's dressed just like any other aspiring PR person would be," Mrs. Mack said, winking at Alex.

"PR person?" Mr. Mack scowled. "I missed something important again, didn't I?"

"It's a new development. Eat."

"Is the car unlocked?" Alex asked, heading for the door to get the box of posters.

Mrs. Mack nodded and Mr. Mack blinked. "She's not taking the car, is she?"

"She doesn't have a license, George. What is it with you tonight?"

Shrugging, Mr. Mack put a piece of pizza on his plate. "Sorry. It's just that Alex looks so— grown-up. I'm not ready."

"You'll get over it." Sighing, Mrs. Mack patted his hand. "If there's one thing we can't stop our children from doing, it's growing up."

Easing out the door, Alex walked toward the car feeling both overjoyed by her dad's reaction and just a little bit sad, too.

Ready or not, she couldn't stop the forward progression of time or the process of becoming an adult.

CHAPTER 7

"Thanks, Mr. Simmons!" Placing a roll of tape in her bag and picking up the few posters she had left, Alex waved at the owner of Main Street Cards & Gifts as she darted through the door. Outside, she paused to glance at the modified poster that now hung in the store's front window beside an array of New Year's Eve party favors, paper table products, and stuffed bears with attached hats and noisemakers. Confetti and long, colorful swirls of narrow, curled ribbon were artistically scattered around the festive items.

The poster fit in perfectly and the colorful marker changes definitely captured the eye. The word "Gala" had been outlined in red followed by exclamation points in blue, yellow, and green. They had also added insert marks, which looked like a pyramid without the bottom line, after the starting and closing times, then written the old and new years' numerals above the marks in different colors. Two additional lines had been written along the lower edge.

Dancing to the wild sounds of ?????
Come and be surprised!

Alex just hoped that whatever group her mom and Mrs. Lincoln found on such short notice wouldn't be an *unpleasant* surprise. She made a mental note to suggest that maybe they should audition anyone who wasn't already booked. CDs would be far better than subjecting the gala-goers to a band that was only marginally competent or worse.

Checking her own reflection in the window glass, Alex smiled. Annie had given her a tailored gray jacket and a light blue blouse to wear with her dark slacks. She looked sharp and professional and headed for Snyder's Pharmacy at the end of the block, convinced that her appearance had made hanging posters easier. The owners and managers of every store she had asked so far had been cooperative and congenial. She would be finished covering the northwest section of city blocks she had been assigned by four o'clock, an hour ahead of schedule. She wondered if the rest of her subcommitte was getting the same response.

Nicole was covering the northeast quadrant of the town, while Ray and Louis covered the south. Robyn had gone to the mall.

"Hey, Robyn!"

At the sound of her name, Robyn stopped dead and turned slowly. Her heart leaped into her throat when she saw Craig Hawkins waving as he hurried toward her. She instantly wondered why. She didn't have a clue, but she was certain there had to be some dreadful reason why the cute new kid on the football team knew her name when they hadn't been introduced.

"Hi, Robyn." Pausing in front of her, Craig smiled. "Man, am I glad to see you."

"You are? Why?" Robyn frowned suspiciously. Then, suddenly recalling Louis's blunt observation and her resulting resolution *not* to assume the worst, she took a mental deep breath and started over. "It's nice to see you, too. We haven't met before, have we?"

"No, but I saw your spot on the news last night. I thought it was great."

"Really?" Robyn caught herself before she began to babble with embarrassed delight at the praise. She had made a favorable impression on the good-looking boy and she didn't want to foul things up on the off chance his interest went beyond simply offering his congratulations. "Thanks."

"You're welcome." Craig paused uncomfortably.

Sensing that he wasn't sure how to keep the conversation going and anxious to keep him talking, Robyn took the initiative. "How do you like Paradise Valley so far?"

"It's okay. I mean, I haven't gotten to know very many people yet."

"Maybe you should come to the New Year's Eve gala." Pulling a poster from the pile she had tucked under her arm, Robyn held it up for inspection. "Most of the kids who aren't out of town for the holidays will be there."

"That's not a bad idea. Maybe I will." Craig glanced at the stack of posters under her arm. "Are you out trying to get these hung up?"

"Yeah." Robyn sighed. "Alex Mack is one of

my best friends and I couldn't say no when she asked me to help."

Craig raised a curious eyebrow. "Alex? Wasn't she one of the girls you interviewed?"

Robyn nodded while hoping the warm flush of excitement spreading across her freckled cheeks wasn't too noticeable. She also didn't want Craig thinking Alex was a total dork the way Charlene Owens had. She had really had to argue to stop Ms. Owens from cutting all of Alex's part from the TV teen segment. Fortunately, Alex hadn't been upset.

"I think Alex was on her way home to get ready for her meeting with the mayor's wife about the gala. That's why she seemed a little out of it. She's really cool."

"I'm sure she is. Could you use some help with those?" Craig glanced at the posters.

"Hanging them?" Robyn's stomach flip-flopped. "Sure!"

Taking the stack of heavy posterboard from Robyn, Craig swept his arm out. "After you."

Her mind racing with the unlikely possibility that this fabulous, soon-to-be-totally-popular new boy might actually be interested in *her*, Robyn started toward The Flower Shoppe with a new spring in her step. She wasn't even worried that she might be exposed to one of the many varieties of blooms that caused her to sneeze uncontrollably.

The power of positive thinking really did work!

Nicole walked into Fins, Feathers, & Fur and came to an abrupt halt. A surge of anger coursed through her as she stared around the pet store.

Rows of tanks full of fish lined the wall on the right. The back section was full of cages with canaries, parakeets, finches, and parrots. Pens stocked with baby rabbits, hamsters, mice, lizards, and snakes were stacked on the wall to the right. Stepping up to the first pen, she looked into the liquid brown eyes of a gray flop-eared bunny. Her heart went out to all the small captive creatures who depended on people for their survival—whether they wanted to or not.

Some, at least, would have the good fortune to end up in homes where they would be properly cared for and loved. *What*, she wondered, *happens to those no one wants?*

"May I help you?"

Eyes flashing, Nicole whirled intending to demand an answer to that disturbing question. It died in her throat as an elderly man with twinkling eyes and rosy cheeks smiled at her, and Louis's words echoed in her thoughts.

There's two sides to every story, Nicole. . . .

"Rabbits require a lot of time and care, you know?" The man leaned over and scratched the little rabbit behind the ears. The animal seemed to welcome his touch and didn't even flinch. "You can't just feed and water them and leave them locked up in a cage. They get lonely just like we do."

"Actually, I just wanted to ask—" Forcing a smile, Nicole held up one of the posters. "—if I could hang this in your front window."

The man studied the poster for a few seconds, then nodded. "Go ahead. If I was fifty years younger, this gala would look like a great way to spend New Year's Eve." Winking, he left to help another customer who had just entered.

Carefully putting easy-remove tabs of tape on the corners of the poster, Nicole placed the advertisement in the lower right corner of the window. She couldn't help overhearing the conversation going on between the store owner and the scruffy-looking middle-aged man in coveralls who was buying a huge bag of dog food.

"Did you ever get those dog runs of yours

cleaned up, Herman?" the elderly store keeper asked with a slight edge of irritation in his voice.

"That's no business of yours, Melvin. My hunting dogs gotta work for their keep. Can't have 'em gettin' soft and lazy on me."

"They'll hunt better if they have clean pens and fresh water," Melvin countered. "And if you're smart, you'll see that they do. Otherwise they just might get taken away when the Humane Society pays you a surprise visit."

"Is that a threat?" Herman scowled menacingly. "I can always take my business somewhere else."

"You could, but I've got the lowest prices in Paradise Valley." Handing the dog owner his change, Melvin smiled. "A word of advice. Get those pens cleaned before the end of the week. Have a nice day."

Nicole sighed as Herman stomped out of the store with the bag of dog food slung over his shoulder. She felt badly for having jumped to a conclusion when she had first come in. Just because a person made his living selling animals didn't mean that person didn't honestly care what happened to them. Melvin really did care, and because of him her resolve to look into both sides of every issue that aroused her became more entrenched.

Nicole left feeling a little foolish and a lot wiser.

"Which way do you want to go?" Louis asked.

Standing on the corner of Eighth Street and Oak, Ray met his friend's pointed gaze. Louis had been baiting him into making all the decisions since they had left the Macks' house. It was getting tiresome, but he was so determined to keep his resolution, Ray didn't hesitate.

"To the right. There's a minimall on the corner of Ninth. A lot of kids go into the convenience store there."

"Works for me."

Ray lengthened his stride as they walked down the sidewalk. They were actually making good time even though they had decided to cover their two quandrants together rather than split up. Louis had argued that a request from two kids to hang the poster would be harder to turn down. Ray suspected Louis just wanted company during the tedious poster trek. So far, no one had objected, and unless they ran into some unforeseen problem, they'd be finished long before the five o'clock debriefing at Alex's house.

"Maybe this isn't such a good idea," Louis said when they reached the corner convenience store.

Looking at the minimarket windows, Ray had to agree. The glass was covered with large ads for store specials and a colorful collection of different-sized posters for other events. The New Year's Eve gala poster would be lost in the confusion.

"What about the bakery next door?" Ray suggested.

"Excellent idea!" Executing an about-face, Louis began to backtrack. "All this walking has made me hungry."

The Ninth Street Bakery was empty. While Louis studied the selection of doughnuts in a glass display case, Ray walked up to the counter and craned his neck to look through the door into the kitchen.

"Hello! Anyone here!"

"Just a minute!" A voice hollered back.

"They must have had a run on chocolate-covered cream-filled today," Louis muttered with a disappointed scowl.

Ray smiled. Gloria always set the last chocolate cream aside for Louis at Wayne's Wigwam in the mall. He didn't think she did it because she knew that was Louis's favorite. She had just gotten tired of listening to him complain if she ran out.

After a couple minutes, a harried-looking woman wearing a white baker's hat and apron entered with a tray of freshly baked doughnuts. "What do you two want?"

Ray hesitated, surprised by the woman's antagonistic tone.

Louis was immune to hostility when his growling stomach was involved. Inhaling the tantalizing aroma wafting from the tray, he pulled a dollar from his pocket. "Two of whatever those are! They smell great."

"Two coconut cream." As the woman pulled a paper from a box on the counter, the phone rang. Rolling her eyes, she answered. "Another hour! Get here as soon as you can, Glen. Sheryl called in sick and we won't have any doughnuts to sell if I can't stay in the kitchen and make them without being interrupted every few minutes!"

Slamming the receiver down, the woman reached into the case for two doughnuts and handed them to Louis. "That'll be eighty-seven cents."

Ray refused the doughnut Louis held out to him, then watched as Louis smiled in anticipation, took a huge bite—and gagged.

"What's wrong?" The baker scowled as she held out Louis's change.

Considering the horrified grimace on Louis's face, the doughnut tasted awful and Ray fully expected Louis to break his resolution in five seconds flat. However, to his surprise, Louis didn't express his disgust in a tactless outspoken burst that was guaranteed to get them thrown out of the store by the insulted woman.

"Uh, gosh." Swallowing with a pained expression, Louis took a deep breath. "I know you've got your hands full here because you don't have any help, but—"

The frantic woman's expression softened as Louis discreetly pointed out the hardships she was working under. "But?"

"I think you left the sugar out of this batch or something," Louis explained with an apologetic shrug.

Ray tensed as the baker took Louis's uneaten doughnut back and risked a hesitant bite. She immediately spat it into a wastepaper can behind the counter.

"Oh, my word! That's terrible! If I had sold these, the phone would have rung off the hook with complaints and there's no telling how many customers I would have lost. I owe you one, kid." Removing the tray from the case, the baker turned toward the kitchen.

"That's okay," Louis said with a cocky wink at Ray. "Although—would it be all right if we hang this poster in your window? It's for the teen New Year's Eve gala the town is sponsoring."

"Go ahead, but don't leave. You've got a couple of deluxe doughnuts coming on the house."

Relaxing as the baker left to dump the spoiled doughnuts, Ray handed Louis a poster and the tape. "You really handled that well, Louis."

"Yeah, I did, didn't I?" Beaming, Louis placed the poster on the glass. "I never realized being nice could be so rewarding. I love bear claws."

When the baker returned, Louis chose a huge bear claw, then watched as Ray studied the assortment of larger, deluxe doughnuts topped with extra icing. Knowing that Louis expected him to pick, then change his selection like he always did when faced with so many delicious choices, Ray pointed to a double-sized, cinnamon-coated, apple-filled doughnut. Without saying so, and maybe without even meaning to, Louis was turning their vow to keep their resolutions into a friendly competition. Ray couldn't resist the unspoken challenge. Although the glazed twists looked good, too, he did not change his mind.

"Have you decided where to go next?" Louis asked as he pocketed his refunded change and held open the door.

"Down Ninth to the Wexford Street Rec Center," Ray said without hesitation. "We'll hang one on the bulletin board in the entry hall."

"You're sure?"

"Positive." Grinning, Ray strode toward the corner. Louis didn't know it, but the future lawyer's determination to make him break his resolution first just made him more determined to stick to it.

After hanging her last poster, Alex decided to check in with her mother and Valerie Lincoln at City Hall. As she had been walking around town, her mind had been working on the decoration problem and she had thought of a great motif that wouldn't cost much and would directly involve all the kids that showed up. She had also come up with a solution to the music problem in the event her mom and Mrs. Lincoln couldn't find a decent band.

Since it was Saturday, City Hall was officially closed again. However, remembering Alex from the day before, the security guard let her in without asking a single question. She found her mother in room 112, hunched over a computer terminal.

"Hi, Mom."

Concentrating so hard that she didn't hear Alex enter, Mrs. Mack jumped with a sharp gasp. "Alex!"

"Sorry. I didn't mean to startle you." Alex sat down at the end of the table. "I just wanted to let you know that everyone's meeting at our house at five to report on the poster distribution, but I'm sure they all got put up okay."

"I didn't have a doubt." Smiling, Mrs. Mack took off her glasses and rubbed her eyes.

"How's the band hunt going?"

"That's Valerie's department, but I don't think she's located anyone yet. I expect her back soon, though. She went to the airport to pick up Mr. Dobbs and his daughter, Kimberly."

"Well, I had an idea—just in case you don't

find anyone. It's not ideal, but in an emergency I think it would work."

Setting her glasses aside and sitting back, Mrs. Mack focused on Alex. "Well, let's hear it. To be honest, I don't think we're going to find anyone worth having at this late date."

Bursting with enthusiasm, Alex leaned forward. "The Community Center has a public address system, right?" When her mother nodded, Alex forged ahead. "Well, it would be easy to hook up a regular CD deck, and between me and my friends, we've got all the latest releases. And it wouldn't cost a cent."

"That's true, but we'd still need a DJ."

"Ray and Louis. They're not professionals, but I think they could do it."

"That's not a bad idea, Alex." Nodding thoughtfully, Mrs. Mack jotted a note on a pad beside the keyboard. "And we won't have to decide until the last minute, either. That is, if they want to do it."

"Knowing Ray and Louis," Alex said confidently, "they'd jump at the chance to be in the spotlight. In fact, they might not even want to be paid!"

Mrs. Mack grinned. "That's fine, but in all fairness, we'd pay them the same thing we had set aside for the band. So you haven't asked them yet?"

Alex shook her head. "I don't want to get their hopes up if it turns out we don't need them."

"Good point." Mrs. Mack frowned when Alex opened her mouth to say something else, then didn't. "What?"

"I, uh—had an idea about the decorations, but—" Sighing, Alex shrugged. "I don't want you to think I'm trying to take over or anything."

"First of all," Mrs. Mack said seriously. "I asked for your input about the decorations. Second, if I don't think your ideas will work for some reason, I'll say so."

"Deal." However, before Alex had a chance to begin, Mrs. Lincoln entered with Mr. Dobbs and his daughter and introduced everyone.

Following Mrs. Mack's lead, Alex stood up and studied the distinguished-looking man as he shook hands with her mother.

"Barbara will be showing you around town and the surrounding area, Mr. Dobbs," Mrs. Lincoln explained. "She'll be able to answer most of your questions and get you any information you might need."

"Excellent." Mr. Dobbs's smile was tight and without humor, and his stiff manner indicated his interest in them and Paradise Valley was strictly business. His fashionably dressed, pretty daughter, Kimberly, just looked bored.

"I'm glad you're here, too, Alexandra," Mrs. Lincoln said. "It would be so nice if you could give Kimberly the guided tour so she can get acquainted with the community from a teenager's perspective."

Although the mayor's wife was still smiling, Alex thought she saw a hint of desperation in her eyes. She couldn't refuse, even though something about the girl made her uncomfortable. She had asked her mother if there was something she could do to help the night before and now Mrs. Lincoln had offered her the chance. An adult did not turn away from a difficult task, especially when it involved doing a favor for a family friend.

"Sure. I'd love to."

Mrs. Lincoln sighed with relief. "Wonderful. After all, if Dobbs Manufacturing builds an auxiliary plant here, Kimberly will be living in Paradise Valley."

Kimberly's eyes flashed. "I have no intention of *ever* living in this backwater burg."

CHAPTER 8

Alex met the girl's hostile gaze without flinching. Inside, she fumed. Paradise Valley was not a huge, cosmopolitan city, but it wasn't a backwater, either. It was just small and geographically isolated.

"Kimberly," Mr. Dobbs said evenly. "I'd like to speak to you a moment, please. In the hall."

Rolling her eyes, Kimberly spun and followed her father out of the room.

Mrs. Lincoln instantly sagged. "That girl is going to be a real problem."

Mrs. Mack frowned uncertainly. "She's obviously spoiled, but I can't believe a successful businessman like Mr. Dobbs would make an important decision, like where to locate his company, based on his daughter's feelings."

Setting her insulted anger aside, Alex listened from a new perspective. She had thought Mrs. Lincoln just wanted her to keep Kimberly occupied while her father conducted his business. Apparently, there was a lot more to it than that.

"Not necessarily." Sighing wearily, Mrs. Lincoln sank into a chair. "Mr. Dobbs intends to move so he can personally supervise building and setting up the new plant. Coming here in the car, I found out that he's been a widower since Kimberly was three. When she complained about moving to a 'cultural wasteland' and leaving her old school and friends, he promised he wouldn't relocate anywhere she didn't like. That's why I was so happy to see you, Alexandra."

Alex blinked.

Mrs. Mack's frown deepened.

"I'm sure you're aware of how important a second major industry could be to our town," Mrs. Lincoln continued. "Mr. Dobbs has already made inquiries about land to buy, but his final decision may rest *entirely* with how Kimberly feels about living in Paradise Valley."

"And you want me to convince her that this is a great place to live?" Alex asked aghast. She thought it was great, but she was pretty sure Kimberly wouldn't.

"That's an awfully big responsibility to put on Alex's shoulders," Mrs. Mack observed.

"I know she can handle it, Barbara." Mrs. Lincoln looked back at Alex. "Just show her what you and your friends do to have fun! In fact—"

As the mayor's wife rose and walked across the room, Alex caught her mother's eye as she started to object again. She stayed her mother's comment with a raised hand. She was pleased that Mrs. Lincoln was entrusting her with a PR assignment that was just as important as her mom's job with Kimberly's father. Committed to keeping her resolution to conduct herself like an adult and genuinely interested in public relations as a possible career, she wanted to follow through.

"Are you sure you really want to do this, Alex?" Mrs. Mack whispered. "I have a feeling spending time with Kimberly won't be pleasant, and she's going to be here a couple of days. Besides, I doubt anything you do will change her mind about Paradise Valley."

Alex whispered back. "If you could handle Danielle Atron's PR account all those years, I think I can handle two days of Kimberly Dobbs. And maybe I will be able to change her mind. Either way, I want to try."

Taking a deep breath, Mrs. Mack nodded as Mrs. Lincoln came back with a fistful of money.

"Barbara, I'd like you and George to join my husband and me for dinner with Mr. Dobbs. Seven o'clock at our house."

"We'll be there."

"And while we're doing that, Alexandra—"

Alex stared at the forty dollars Mrs. Lincoln put in her hand. "What's this?"

"Petty cash from the city's PR budget. I want you to take Kimberly out for pizza or something with your friends who helped with the posters."

"And don't forget to bring back the receipt." Mrs. Mack winked.

"Cool!" Thrilled, Alex quickly exchanged her smile for a look of composure as Mr. Dobbs and Kimberly came back in.

After Mrs. Lincoln outlined the dinner plans and Mr. Dobbs accepted without giving his sullen daughter a chance to argue, Mrs. Mack spoke up.

"Why don't you ride home with Alex and me now, Kimberly? If it's all right with your father, of course."

"To be honest, Mrs. Mack," Kimberly said— politely, but not at all happily, "I'd really rather—"

"She'd be glad to." Mr. Dobbs finished for her.

"Yes." Kimberly sighed, apparently not daring to contradict her father, who had obviously instructed her to mind her manners when they were in the hall. "I'd love to."

Hoping she hadn't bitten off a whole lot more than she could chew, Alex hid her dislike and tried to break the ice. However, bearing in mind Kimberly's snobbish attitude, she kept her tone and expression even and slightly remote. "My friends will be meeting us at the house and we can go to eat from there."

"Just as long as it's not pizza," Kimberly said with disdain. "I hate pizza."

As Mr. Dobbs and his daughter turned to leave, Alex almost broke out laughing when she saw her mom and Mrs. Lincoln both roll *their* eyes.

*   *   *

Alone in the ladies room of Chop Suey Louie's, Alex took a few minutes to brace herself
for the next round of Kimberly versus Paradise
Valley. She had never realized how much diplo-
macy entered into being a good public relations
agent. Or how strenuous figuring out how to
keep everyone happy and on speaking terms
could be. The enormous respect she felt for her
mother, who had been a PR account executive
for years, rose by several notches.

When a customer came in to wash her hands,
Alex locked herself in one of the two stalls and
took several deep breaths. She had almost
botched the whole assignment several times already, and the only way she had saved it was
by acting like a complete jerk.

Suddenly everything went dark as the woman
flicked off the light switch on her way out.

Alex sighed. Her decline into the darker pits
of PR work had started in the car on the way
home when Kimberly had asked what clothing
stores Paradise Valley had to offer. Her mother
had looked at Alex as if she were a total stranger
when she answered.

*"The mall is small but totally exclusive. Strictly
top designer labels."*

Alex groaned just thinking about it. The worst thing was that Kimberly had immediately warmed up.

Then, when they pulled into the driveway, they had run into Annie on her way out to go bowling with friends. That was the latest in a growing list of "normal" activities her brilliant sister was determined to experience because she had spent most of her time in high school studying instead of having fun.

"Bowling? How totally crude. Your sister obviously doesn't have your class, Alex."

"My sister is a genius, Kimberly. She's doing a research paper for a physics course at MIT on . . . the dynamics of bowling for the purpose of measuring impact energies as they apply to meteors hitting Earth."

Her defensive explanation had been total gibberish. Fortunately, Kimberly spent more time studying her horoscope than she did science and was impressed. Alex felt guilty because she had made excuses for Annie, who was brilliant and didn't need to apologize to anyone because she wanted to go bowling.

Alex opened the stall door, zapped the light back on, then let the door slam closed. Worn out and stressed, she assured herself that not wanting to sit in the dark was no more frivolous than saving a pizza on the brink of certain destruction. Using her powers had saved time and energy and had taken some of the edge off her frayed nerves. Her troubles hadn't ended with defending Annie.

After finding out that Kimberly was health conscious in the extreme and in the habit of hanging out at a fancy gourmet restaurant, there was no question that the girl would despise the local teens' favorite café. Alex had had to deftly maneuver them into splurging on something to eat other than pizza and going somewhere besides the Half-Life before she was able to tell them that impressing Kimberly might be vital to the town.

"I've got great news! The city's buying everyone dinner. Why don't we take the opportunity to try that new gourmet restaurant on Warner?"

"That upwardly mobile place that charges a fortune for dinky portions of stuff I never heard of?" Nicole asked with a deadpan expression that didn't quite betray her loathing of pretention.

"Spoons on the Side," Louis scoffed. *"I'd rather have—"*

"Italian?" Alex cut him off with a quick glance at Kimberly, who wore a smile of amused superiority.

"I'm allergic to oregano," Robyn said.

"You have allergies, too?" Craig asked.

"Chinese," Ray suggested.

The essence of Kimberly's smile changed when she looked at Ray. *"I love Chinese."*

Alex didn't know if Kimberly Dobbs really liked Chinese food or if she was just interested in Ray, but everyone was in unanimous agreement. Now they were all seated around a huge round table at Chop Suey Louie's, waiting for her.

Suddenly aware of the troublesome twists the conversation could take without her there to run interference, Alex quickly returned to the dining room. She couldn't ignore her responsibility to her mother and Mrs. Lincoln just because she wasn't comfortable with the tactics she'd had to use. The future of Paradise Valley might depend on whether Kimberly liked or disliked it. And *that* depended on *her.*

Alex was relieved to find that no one at the table seemed upset, probably because the group was still discussing what to order and hadn't hit on other more touchy subjects—yet. In spite of their resolutions, Nicole and Louis might not be able to curb their reactions to Kimberly's arrogant attitude. Robyn was obviously captivated by Craig Hawkins and too preoccupied to notice Kimberly's barely concealed contempt for the town. Still, that was also a potentially explosive situation, too. Recalling how Craig had questioned Kelly about *her* identity the night before, Alex couldn't help but wonder about his motives for latching onto Robyn, especially since he kept looking at her across the table. Ray, on the other hand, was giving Kimberly his undivided attention.

"General Tso's chicken is spicy," Ray explained. "It's got a zing, but it won't burn your mouth like the Szechuan style."

"You decide, Ray." Sighing with exaggerated weariness, Kimberly leaned closer to him. "I'm too exhausted after my trip."

Alex caught the "is-she-real?" look Nicole cast her way, and shrugged.

"All right." Ray closed his menu. "General Tso's chicken and beef with scallops for us."

"You're sure?" Louis peered at him pointedly.

"Positive." Ray stared back.

Looking up after conferring with Robyn, Craig announced that they had finally settled on sweet and sour pork and chicken. "Neither of us is sensitive to sweet and sour. What are you having, Alex?''

"I haven't decided yet." Realizing she had sounded annoyed, Alex smiled to cover the slip. It was a perfectly reasonable, friendly question. "Everything sounds good.''

Craig grinned back.

After they had ordered, Alex focused the conversation on a discussion of life in Paradise Valley for the benefit of both newcomers. While Craig questioned everything with curious interest, Kimberly only offered an occasional subtly sarcastic or derogatory comment. Like Kelly Phillips, Kimberly had perfected the craft of being scornful, so it was difficult to tell if that's what she intended. By the time they were finished eating, Alex couldn't wait to call it a night. However, no one else was in a hurry to leave.

"It's hard to believe you two just met,'' Kimberly said in reference to Robyn and Craig.

"I know,'' Robyn said with a shy smile at the boy. "We seem to have a lot in common.''

"What?'' Louis asked. "Besides your allergies?'' He flinched when Nicole nudged him, then muttered, "That *wasn't* tactless.''

Hopelessly infatuated, Robyn didn't take of-

fense. "Craig is thinking about a career in broadcasting, too. As a sportscaster."

"But you're such a good football player,
Craig." Ray looked bewildered. "I would have
thought you'd want to play pro ball—not report it."

Craig smiled. "I'd rather have a career that
doesn't involve broken bones and I probably
wouldn't last beyond the age of thirty. If I was
lucky."

Kimberly arched an eyebrow and addressed
Robyn. "You don't strike me as someone who'd
be interested in sportscasting. I mean, you don't
look—athletic."

"Hardly. But I'm seriously considering broadcast journalism, which is almost the same."

"She already has her own show," Ray said.

"Sort of," Nicole corrected. "She's doing a
weekly teen spot for Channel Eleven."

"If I can come up with a topic for next week."
Robyn's smile faded into a brief frown before
she realized her pessimistic nature was showing.
"And I'm sure I will!"

"Why not cover the New Year's Eve gala?"
Alex suggested, jumping on the opportunity to
wangle a plug for the event.

"That's an idea." Robyn nodded.

"Or you could do something on what kids think about the plant Kimberly's father might build," Ray said.

Perking up, Robyn smiled. "That might work. I know Charlene Owens is planning to do a story about it. Maybe I could interview you, Kimberly."

"Me?" Kimberly's eyes widened with surprise and delight. "I've always wanted to be interviewed."

As much as Alex wanted the publicity for the gala, Kimberly's response to Robyn's offer was the first sign of genuine enthusiasm she had detected for anything or anyone in Paradise Valley besides Ray. The Dobbs Manufacturing plant was a lot more important than a teen dance.

"What exactly does Dobbs Manufacturing manufacture?" Nicole asked casually.

"Plastic gizmos for automobiles," Kimberly answered, looking bored. "Valves or couplings. Something like that. I'm not exactly sure."

"All those little things that break and are expensive to replace—uh!" Louis scowled at Alex, but he shut up.

Alex justified gently kicking him under the table because he had come very close to breaking his resolution by almost insulting Kimberly. She started to change the subject, but Nicole was one step ahead of her again.

"Making plastics creates a lot of toxic by-products. Is your dad planning to install state-of-the-art equipment to prevent pumping dangerous pollutants into the air?"

"I'm sure he is," Kimberly bristled. "Within reason. One thing I do know is that if the cost of making the gizmos gets too high, he'll lose his contracts."

"And people would be out of jobs," Ray added.

"Yes. That's quite true, Ray. And no company stays in business long without a decent profit margin."

"Having a *second* industry in town would really boost the town's economy, not to mention the other benefits," Alex observed. "Right now, almost everyone is totally dependent on Paradise Valley Chemical."

Everyone nodded. No one had forgotten how dismal things were in Paradise Valley last Christmas when it looked as if the chemical plant was going to have major layoffs. Alex's father had developed an effective acne medicine that had saved the company and everyone's jobs. Still, it had been a close call.

"I suppose," Nicole grumbled, making an effort to take all aspects of the situation into consideration.

Robyn pulled a small notebook out of her purse and quickly wrote a few notes.

Alex suspected that Kimberly wasn't as interested in keeping people employed as she was in maintaining her own lifestyle. She didn't say so, but used the sudden silence to steer the talk to safer ground. "We'd love to have you come to the gala if you can arrange it, Kimberly."

"There's a thought." Kimberly nodded. "I haven't been able to make any definite plans because of all this traveling around with Dad. He wants to close the deal on the land before the end of the year, if possible."

Close the deal? Alex frowned slightly. According to Mrs. Lincoln, Mr. Dobbs was just making inquiries.

"Alex's mom has lined up a great band called—what?" Ray looked at Alex in confusion as she shook her head.

"Backward Time canceled," Alex explained reluctantly.

"That's a bummer." Craig frowned. "They're getting to be known all over the state. It's only a matter of time before they hit nationally."

"So who's gonna play instead?" Robyn asked.

"We're working on it." Alex smiled tightly.

"You don't have anyone yet?" Louis blinked, shocked.

"Actually," Kimberly interjected, "that's something I might be able to help you with."

"How?" Alex asked. Aside from solving the music problem, connecting Kimberly with the gala was a way to use Robyn's weekly teen segment for both.

"Well—" Leaning forward, Kimberly exhibited another burst of real enthusiasm. "My dad always has a huge formal house party on New Year's Eve and he always hires Chuck Cassidy's ballroom band. But since Dad's not doing it this year and Mr. Cassidy never books his band anywhere else on New Year's Eve, he's probably free to play your gala! I bet my dad would even pay for it."

"He would?" Alex asked, her interest mounting.

Kimberly nodded. "He feels guilty for not letting them know he didn't need them sooner so they could get another gig."

"Formal?" Nicole started.

"Ballroom band?" Ray frowned slightly.

"What's wrong?" Kimberly glanced at Alex.

"I just assumed this was a formal affair. It *is* New Year's Eve."

Scanning her friends' puzzled and distressed faces, Alex valiantly tried to bridge the widening gap between them and Kimberly. "Why not formal? The high school proms always are, and no one objects to that."

"We just finished putting the posters up all over town." Louis tensed, waiting for someone to nudge him again, then relaxed when no one did.

"It wouldn't be *that* hard to change them. . . ." Ray was thinking out loud, but Kimberly took his comment as agreement and turned it to her advantage.

"An excellent suggestion, Ray. Alex was going to show me around, but she's *so* busy with the gala. If I help you alter the posters, I'd see Paradise Valley *and* have a chance to get to know you better."

Ray hesitated uncertainly, then grinned broadly. "Sounds like a plan to me."

Nicole sighed.

Louis raised a quizzical eyebrow. "Does this mean the New Year's Eve gala is now a formal dance with a ballroom band that thinks alternative music is a jitterbug instead of a waltz?"

When everyone turned to look at him, Louis shrugged. "Just asking."

"Yes, it is." Alex was sure neither her mother nor Mrs. Lincoln would object, especially since her sudden decision might have tipped the scales in favor of Paradise Valley as far as Kimberly was concerned.

"Fab!" Beaming at Ray, Kimberly possessively slipped her arm through his. "I'll have to go shopping for something absolutely smashing to wear."

No one else, including Ray, was even remotely thrilled. Alex didn't blame them. With a split-second decision, she had turned their chance to bring in the New Year with energetic and enthusiastic fun into a dull formal dance with obsolete music no one but Kimberly would enjoy.

Alex doubted that any of the local teens would appreciate the change. A lot of them might not even come. However, that was secondary to having Dobbs Manufacturing move to the area. Since Kimberly's father wanted to close his land deal before the first, it wouldn't matter if the gala was a total flop. By then, it would be too late for Kimberly to change her mind.

And if he didn't close the deal before the dance, maybe Kimberly would think Paradise

Valley just had a small, but cultured, teenaged population.

Breaking Danielle Atron's hold on the town would be worth it either way, Alex told herself. Even if none of her friends ever spoke to her again.

CHAPTER 9

"A formal dance?" Mrs. Mack looked up from her morning coffee to stare at Alex across the kitchen table. Since it was Sunday, Annie and Mr. Mack were sleeping in. "Are you sure that's what you really want?"

Alex sighed. "No, it's not what I want. Neither do my friends. It's what Kimberly wants. And if we don't agree to hold the kind of dance Kimberly wants, Paradise Valley might not get the second major industry *it* wants."

"Unfortunately, that's one of the down sides of public relations work, Alex. I can't tell you how many times I had to compromise my own principles to keep Danielle Atron happy."

Alex sighed again. "At least Kimberly's pretty sure her father will pay to bring in a ballroom band he knows. She'll call me later."

"Well, that's something, I guess. Let Valerie know right away, okay? Having the band set will be one less thing to worry about. Besides, she wants to talk to you about your decorating idea."

Alex still hadn't told her mother what her idea was, but it probably didn't matter now, anyway. "I'm not sure what I had in mind will work for a formal dance, but I'll call her. I did remember to get the receipt for dinner last night."

Mrs. Mack gave her a thumbs-up. "Great. Maybe you'd better put it in my purse, though. So *I* don't forget to hand it in. This Dobbs business has got me totally preoccupied."

"Sure. How's it going?" Alex asked.

"Fine. I think." Taking a deep breath, Mrs. Mack sighed with the same frustration Alex felt. "There's something about this whole new plant project that bothers me, but I can't quite put my finger on it."

"You must have some clue, Mom."

"No, I don't. On the surface, everything Mr. Dobbs is proposing seems in order. The mayor and the city council are absolutely determined to get that new plant because it means jobs and will benefit every business in town. It's almost too good to be true."

"Well, you know what they say about that." Alex looked at her pointedly. "If it *seems* too good to be true, it probably is."

After conveying Kimberly's message that Chuck Cassidy's ballroom band was booked for the gala, and getting the go-ahead from Mrs. Lincoln on her decorating idea, Alex spent all day Sunday on the telephone tracking down the necessary supplies. She was thrilled that the mayor's wife thought her original idea would add a certain intellectual flair to the now-formal gathering.

Using huge precut numbers, sections of the Community Center walls would be set aside for time periods dating back to the mid-1800s. Although the town of Paradise Valley hadn't been incorporated and developed until Paradise Valley Chemical opened fifteen years before, the area had a rich history. Pictures and mementos from the historical society, the library, the *Paradise Valley Press*, and City Hall would show life in Paradise Valley in the past. The end wall would be kept blank with numbers for the current year and the year to come. The kids who attended the event would have a chance to post pictures they cut from stacks of donated magazines that symbolized things that had happened this year and what they hoped would happen next year. Track lighting that was already installed would allow the display to be seen even though most of the room would be dimmed to a more appropriate level for a dance. The Women's Auxiliary had agreed to put up the historical display, and in keeping with the formal nature of the event, they would also decorate the tables with bud vases, tablecloths, glass candles and typical New Year's Eve party favors.

And, Alex thought proudly as she waited for Robyn and Nicole late Monday morning, *Mrs. Lincoln is so impressed she wants to keep the display open for public viewing the whole following week!*

Expecting the two girls, who were going to help her collect the wall hangings and magazines from the various donors, Alex was surprised to find Ray waiting on the porch when the doorbell rang.

"Help!" With a look of total desperation, Ray dashed inside, glanced furtively over his shoulder, then slammed the door closed.

"What's wrong?" Alex cautiously peered out

the front window. Robyn and Nicole were on their way up the front walk, but no one else was in sight.

"If it's Kimberly, don't open it!" Ray waved his hands in a near panic.

"It's just Robyn and Nicole." Worried and wondering what Kimberly had done to turn the easygoing, usually unflustered Ray into a basket case, Alex opened the door for the girls.

"We've got to talk, Alex." Without looking at her, Nicole stormed inside. Robyn followed carrying a pad and pen.

"What's wrong with Nicole?" Alex whispered to Robyn as their angry friend began to pace in the living room.

"She's looked at both sides of the Dobbs Manufacturing issue and finally decided that there must be something rotten on the Dobbs side." Robyn graced Alex with a pained but valiant smile. "As for myself, I'm optimistically hoping to get a great story. I hate to say it, Alex, but you could be in big trouble for aiding and abetting the enemy."

Stunned, Alex hesitated as Robyn went in to join Nicole and Ray. When she finally started to close the door, it met with another powerful force coming from the opposite direction. Stumbling backward when Louis burst in, Alex just blinked as he confronted Ray.

"I don't care if she is driving you nuts, Ray! You've got to talk to Kimberly so she stops calling me! My phone's been ringing off the hook all morning."

"No way!" Ray held up his hands. "She's determined to wear me down so I'll ask her to go to the gala as my date. If I talk to her, I might break!"

"But aren't you two supposed to be changing the posters so everyone knows the gala is formal?" Robyn asked.

"We finished that at two o'clock yesterday afternoon." Sighing despondently, Ray collapsed on the couch. "Then we went to every art gallery in town and every gallery served expresso, which Kimberly insisted we just had to try. According to her, none of them were very good. My stomach is in total agreement."

"Well, you asked for it, Ray," Nicole said unsympathetically. "She's pretty and she pushed all your macho buttons with those big brown eyes of hers."

"I did *not* ask to be dragged to a sappy French double feature with subtitles!" Crossing his arms, Ray exhaled loudly. "I only agreed to let her help me with the posters."

"Then why didn't you ditch her when you were through?" Dropping down on the couch, Louis stared at Ray. "Sometimes you just have to be ruthless."

"*This* was *not* one of those times," Ray said defensively. "I let her hang with me because Alex said the future of Paradise Valley depends on keeping Kimberly happy."

"It does," Nicole said coldly. "But that future may not necessarily be one that *benefits* Paradise Valley."

"What do you mean?" Alex asked. She had been on the verge of suggesting that maybe Ray should take Kimberly to the dance.

"I mean that Dobbs Manufacturing may not care about the town's best interests in connection with that plant." Nicole's barely controlled temper flashed. "I just can't believe you'd help someone who wants to ruin our community, Alex!"

"I'm not helping Mr. Dobbs," Alex explained calmly. Since she obviously hadn't made it clear she was working for the city, she couldn't blame Nicole for being angry and upset. "Mrs. Lincoln asked me to show Kimberly around because the city council is convinced having another industry will be good for the town. If you know for a fact that Mr. Dobbs plans to do something that will hurt Paradise Valley, I've got to know so I can alert my mom."

"Gosh, I'm sorry, Alex. I should have known you wouldn't turn traitor on us." Sagging, Nicole sat down on the floor.

"Well, there goes my 'local girl sells out Paradise Valley' story." Sitting down beside Nicole, Robyn patted the carpet. "Come on, Alex. There's got to be another angle to this situation I can work with."

"I'm sure there is." Wearing a dark midcalf-length skirt over high boots with a short-sleeved shirt and a forest green sweater vest, Alex carefully lowered herself to the floor and tucked her legs underneath her. At the moment, she could care less if her good clothes got wrinkled. "What did you find out about Mr. Dobbs, Nicole?"

Nicole looked up sharply and blinked. "Nothing specific. It's just a hunch."

Alex's heart sank.

"Watch it, Nicole," Louis warned. "Sounds to me like you're on the verge of breaking your resolution."

"Not really," Nicole countered. "I resolved to

consider both sides—not accept them. And Kimberly said some things that made me suspicious. Like when I asked her about environmental safeguards. 'Within reason' for whom? I know how corporations operate, and believe me, Dobbs will not install any antipollution equipment in that plant beyond what he needs to satisfy government standards. And that won't be enough."

"There was something else, too," Alex said. "The mayor's wife doesn't know Mr. Dobbs may be ready to close a land deal. She thinks he's just looking."

"See?" Nicole nodded curtly.

"But I'm afraid a hunch and buying land aren't enough to stop the city council from letting Mr. Dobbs build." Alex didn't want to be so negative, but she had to be realistic. Her mother needed evidence that the Dobbs Manufacturing plant would ultimately harm Paradise Valley before she could take action. "My mom thinks there's something fishy about this plan, too, but she can't get a handle on it, either."

"I think Nicole and your mom may be right, Alex." Robyn frowned thoughtfully. "After I taped her interview early this morning, Kimberly said something odd to *me* when I told her Paradise Valley didn't have a performing arts center or an art museum."

"What?" Everyone asked simultaneously.

Imitating Kimberly's contemptuous tone and affected gestures, Robyn repeated what the girl had said. "No matter. When my father gets through with this town, it won't be a backwater burg anymore."

"I should have told her to stuff it last night like I wanted to." Louis sighed. "You know, sometimes being outspoken has its advantages."

"I suppose, but Kimberly is the least of our problems," Nicole said firmly. "We've got to stop her father."

"And how are we supposed to do that?" Louis threw up his hands.

"I could tell Kimberly I think she's a boring, arrogant snob. She'll get mad and that will be that." Ray brightened, then frowned again. "Except she's leaving this afternoon to go home and she won't be back until Wednesday night just before the gala starts. She wants to shop for her dress at some exclusive place because the stores here are 'totally off the rack.' "

Louis picked up the cordless phone from the end table. "So call her at the hotel and tell her."

Alex took the phone. "Bad idea. We can't say

or do *anything* to alienate Kimberly until we know for *sure* the new plant poses a threat to the town." She didn't like having to curb everyone's outraged desire to save Paradise Valley, but nothing would be gained if they deliberately ruined Mr. Dobbs's land deal and made accusations without proof.

"Where exactly is this land Mr. Dobbs is planning to buy?" Robyn asked.

Alex blinked. "I don't know."

"Maybe we should find out," Nicole said. "Call me paranoid, but the fact that we *don't* know strikes me as suspicious. What's the big secret?"

"Maybe it isn't a secret, but I'll ask my mom." Standing up, Alex smoothed the creases out of her skirt. "Right now, though, we've really got to get started collecting that memorabilia for the gala. Annie will drive us, but it may take awhile to get everything together at the different stops."

"Craig wanted to help, but he had some things to do at home." Robyn's eyes sparkled.

"Has he asked you to go to the dance with him?" Nicole asked expectantly.

"Not yet." Robyn sighed. "I could be wrong, but I'm not sure his interest in me is what I thought it was."

"Did something happen?" Alex winced slightly.

"No." Robyn forced a smile. "He's been totally nice. It's probably just my natural inclination to be pessimistic getting in the way again."

Alex couldn't help but wonder if in this case, Robyn's natural inclination to expect the worst might not be better. If Robyn assumed Craig didn't like her the way she did him and she was wrong, she wouldn't be hurt at all. However, if she assumed he shared her feelings and then found out he didn't, the pain and disappointment would be far worse.

And she had to guard against making false assumptions, too, Alex realized with a start. Except for the exchange between Craig and Kelly at the Half-Life, there was no evidence whatsoever that Craig had an ulterior motive for hanging out with Robyn beyond getting to know her and her friends.

"What are you two going to do?" Nicole asked Ray and Louis.

Rising, Ray stretched and sighed. "Well, since we need information and Kimberly is one of our best possible sources, I guess I'll drop by her hotel to say good-bye."

"I think I'd better come with you," Louis said.

"Just so you don't get carried away with your mission and ask her to the dance."

"Good idea." Ray shrugged sheepishly.

"I think it would be a good idea if we all kept our eyes and ears open," Nicole suggested.

Alex had to agree. Just like Robyn's situation with Craig, if they investigated and found out that Dobbs Manufacturing didn't plan to do anything that would ultimately be bad for the community, no harm would be done. But if the opposite was true and they *didn't* check into it, Paradise Valley might never recover from the disastrous consequences of letting Mr. Dobbs build his new plant.

CHAPTER 10

By late Tuesday afternoon, all the historical pictures and mementos had been collected and deposited at the Community Center along with stacks of magazines, scissors, and rolls of tape for the "this year/next year" panel the kids would put up during the gala. However, no one had found out anything concrete about Mr. Dobbs's intentions regarding the town and his plant.

Including the location of the proposed site.

Walking toward City Hall to check in with Mrs. Lincoln about any last-minute details, Alex reviewed the conversation she had had with her mother the night before.

"I'm worried, too, Alex, but Mr. Dobbs doesn't have to tell the city what land he wants to buy."

"But he can't build a plant on it without city approval can he?"

"No, he can't, but—" Sighing, Mrs. Mack rested her chin on her hand. *"I don't think Mr. Dobbs has a problem there, either. All the mayor and the city council seem to care about is jobs and revenues that don't depend on Paradise Valley Chemical."*

Or Danielle Atron, Alex added in her own mind. Her mother hadn't been that specific, but that's what she had meant.

Ray had come up empty yesterday, too. He and Louis had suffered through a long lunch at the hotel's fine-dining restaurant before Kimberly's father had whisked her off to the airport in a rented car. Their description of the ordeal was still vivid in Alex's memory.

"No, the food was great!" Louis shrugged. *"But the dishes and stuff were sooo fancy, I was so afraid of breaking something, I couldn't really enjoy it."*

"Listening to Kimberly insult you so you weren't quite sure that you were being insulted turned my stomach sour," Ray said.

"Listening to her sweet-talk you for two hours didn't sit well on mine, either."

"You didn't do anything you'll regret, did you?"

Alex shifted her gaze from Louis to Ray. "Like insulting her back or asking her to the dance?"

"Actually, as hard as it is to believe, no counterinsults passed my lips." Louis grinned mischievously. "But I only resolved to hold my tongue until midnight tomorrow."

Ray nodded. "The only bright spot in this for me is that I decided not to ask Kimberly to the dance, and I didn't. The worst of it is, every time we tried to get her to talk about her father's business plans in Paradise Valley, she changed the subject."

Alex sighed. The prospects of finding out anything useful about Dobbs Manufacturing before it was too late seemed hopeless. It was possible she was worrying about nothing, but like Nicole and her mom, she just couldn't shake the feeling that something was terribly wrong.

Taking a shortcut across the parking lot, Alex turned to go in the side door just as her mother and Mr. Dobbs were coming out. Both of them had car keys in their hands. Acting on instinct, Alex ducked behind the passenger side of the nearest car. Mr. Dobbs himself might be the only source of the information they needed and she didn't want to be seen in case she got an opportunity to follow him. It was a foolish chance to take, especially since it might be a dead end, but it was the only chance she had.

"I appreciate everything you've done." Holding the door open, Mr. Dobbs let Mrs. Mack walk outside ahead of him. "But you're tired and so am I. Let's just call it a day."

Although her mother smiled, Alex could tell she wasn't happy.

"The City Planning Department will be open for another half hour. I thought you might want to make sure there weren't any restrictions on the property you're buying."

Smart, Mom, Alex thought. To check for restrictions, Mr. Dobbs would have to tell someone in the planning department the location. But he evaded the suggestion.

"That I'm *thinking* about buying," Mr. Dobbs corrected. "And I assure you, I've done my homework. There's no problem."

Defeated, Mrs. Mack just nodded.

Her mom was obviously disappointed but she had the good sense to avoid arguing with a company head who was used to having his orders obeyed.

"Go home and relax. I'm going back to my hotel to do just that. Room service and TV."

"Very well. Until tomorrow, then." Graciously

taking her leave, Mrs. Mack started toward her car, which was parked on the far side of the lot.

Alex held her breath as Mr. Dobbs opened the driver's-side door of the car she was crouched behind. He slid into the front seat, but he didn't close the door or start the engine. Looking under the car, Alex saw his feet planted on the pavement.

What's he waiting for?

As soon as her mother drove away, Alex heard the musical tones of a cellular phone being dialed. Mr. Dobbs was probably just calling Kimberly to check in, she mused, but it seemed more likely that he was making a call he didn't want anyone to overhear. Alex smiled. Mr. Dobbs didn't have a clue that the only kid in the world who could turn into a puddle and listen in was lurking on the other side of his car.

Although eavesdropping was not something she felt comfortable doing, Alex didn't see that she had any choice. There was nothing trivial about using her powers when the fate of the whole town was at stake, either.

Checking to make sure no one could see her, Alex morphed. The warm tingling that started in her toes and radiated throughout her whole body just before she became a liquid seemed to take forever. The instant the transformation was complete, she slithered under the car and puddled behind Mr. Dobbs's perfectly polished shoes.

"It's Dobbs, Mr. Ordway. Do you have the papers ready?" He paused. "Excellent. I'll meet you at the site in a few minutes. If everything's in order, we can close the deal tomorrow afternoon."

Bingo!

Mr. Ordway's name sounded familiar, but Alex didn't know why. She also didn't have time to worry about it. As Mr. Dobbs swung his legs inside the car, she silently oozed into the back. Pooling on the floor behind the front seat, she shimmered as he slammed the car door closed. She could only hope that Mr. Dobbs was so intent on getting to his secret meeting, he wouldn't notice the puddle sloshing around behind him.

Luck was on her side. After Mr. Dobbs put the car in gear and pulled out of the lot, he slipped a classical music CD into the player and turned the volume up. Then the refined and serious man behind the steering wheel began to sing along in a booming off-key voice.

"Dah-da-da-dah-daah! Dah-da-da-dah-daah . . ."

Alex would have smiled if she had a mouth and if the situation wasn't so dire.

Several minutes later, the ride got very bumpy when Mr. Dobbs pulled the car off the main road. Alex tried to muffle her gurgled grunts and she was relieved when Mr. Dobbs suddenly turned the music off and the car jolted to a stop.

Alex waited until Mr. Dobbs opened the car door, stepped out, and walked away across what appeared to be an open field. The shock she felt when she slithered out of the car a moment later and realized where she was almost jolted her into instantaneously transforming back into a girl. Appalled, she stared at the towering fir tree in the town park about half a mile away, remembering why she knew the name Ordway. Ordway's Range was a large, undeveloped section of land that bordered one end of the park and served as an unofficial wildlife preserve.

And Mr. Dobbs was planning to buy the acreage and build a factory on it!

Elongating and moving swiftly through the tall grass, Alex paused a few feet away from where Mr. Dobbs and an old man with a sun-weathered face and a cowboy hat perched on his bald head were talking.

Neatly folding the papers Mr. Ordway handed

him, Mr. Dobbs placed them in an inside pocket of his suit coat, then held out his hand. "What time can I expect you at the real-estate agent's office tomorrow afternoon?"

"When I get there." Grinning impishly, the old man shook Mr. Dobbs's hand, then walked back to his old pickup truck, whistling.

Shaking his head, Mr. Dobbs whipped out his cellular phone and dialed as he wandered back toward his car.

Although it would be dark soon, Alex was worried about morphing back to normal out in the open. Although she could stay morphed a lot longer now, she was pushing the limit. She followed Mr. Dobbs at a distance that allowed her to hear, but was still far enough away to hide her in the twilight shadows of the tall weeds if she couldn't maintain her liquid state.

"We're all set here, Campfield. After I buy this land tomorrow, we can start breaking ground for the new facility." Mr. Dobbs frowned as he listened to the person on the other end. "I already told the architect not to worry about designing space for anything except what's necessary to fulfill the government's minimum environmental requirements."

Alex quivered with a rising anger. Nicole had

been absolutely right. Not only was Mr. Dobbs planning to destroy the country landscape and wildlife habitat that adjoined the park, he didn't care if he poisoned the atmosphere around Paradise Valley!

"No, I haven't told anyone we're relocating our entire operation. Believe me, between the construction boom to build houses for all the employees we'll be moving in and the extra taxes they can collect from us, the Paradise Valley City Council won't care that there won't be many job openings for the town's current residents."

No jobs, either!

Alex flattened herself to the ground when she felt the prickling sensation alerting her that she was about to change into a solid. Luck was still with her, though. Mr. Dobbs got back into his car just as she shifted into human form again.

"I also want you to call Frank at Grimes Construction Enterprises and let him know what's happening. This little town will be ripe for commerical development after we double the population, and I want his company in on it from the start. I own a major percentage of their stock and this opportunity should send the value soaring." Mr. Dobbs nodded enthusiastically. "Another mall at the very least. If Frank wants to talk, I'll be at my hotel all night."

Signing off, Mr. Dobbs closed the car door, turned on his music, and drove away with a satisfied smile.

Sitting up when the car turned back onto the main road, Alex drew her legs under her and stared at the darkening silhouette of the tall fir in the park. Last Christmas she and Ray had strung all the tree's lights in the middle of the night, then paid for forty-six minutes of electrical power to run them because Paradise Valley Chemical's shaky financial situation had prevented Danielle Atron from paying the bill as usual. The lighted tree had filled everyone in town with the spirit of the season in spite of their troubles.

Now, Paradise Valley faced an even worse fate—the total destruction of its small-town charm when Dobbs Manufacturing moved in and brought with it the blight of uncontrolled suburban sprawl. Everything that made the community a wonderful and unique place to live would be gone, swallowed up by more housing developments, minimalls, gas stations, restaurants, and bigger highways to handle all the traffic an increased population would create.

Unless someone did something about it.

The distant giant fir tree suddenly blazed with ten thousand glittering Christmas lights, filling Alex with inspired determination.

She hadn't given up trying to save Christmas in Paradise Valley last year against seemingly hopeless odds.

No way was she going to give up trying to save Paradise Valley itself now.

Rising and dusting herself off, Alex boldly strode across the field toward home. The game was not over yet and she had three aces to play.

Her mother.

Robyn.

And Danielle Atron.

CHAPTER 11

Everyone seated in the Wilsons' family room reacted as though Alex had just announced that Paradise Valley was about to be invaded by aliens.

Nicole gasped.

Ray and Louis blinked in disbelief.

Robyn scribbled furiously on her pad.

Craig's stare was blank with shock.

Having reported everything she had found out from Mr. Dobbs's telephone conversations, Alex gave them all a few moments to absorb the unsettling news and recover. Everyone had accepted that she had overheard him talking on his cell phone at City Hall, which was close to being true.

Her mother had gone directly to bed when she had gotten home and was sound asleep before Alex arrived. Since her mom wouldn't be able to do anything until City Hall opened in the morning anyway, she had decided to let her rest. Annie and her father had gone to see a movie together and had left a note saying they wouldn't be back until late. Desperate and ready for action, Alex had called an emergency meeting of her friends. They had decided to meet at Nicole's so they wouldn't disturb Mrs. Mack.

"We can*not* let that happen!" Craig's eyes gleamed with angry indignation. "My dad decided to open a dry cleaning business here because he wanted to live somewhere that wasn't turning into a generic community that looked and felt like a hundred others."

"How can the mayor and the city council sleep nights knowing they're selling out the town?" Nicole snapped.

"I don't think they have all the facts," Alex countered. "From what I've heard, they're under the impression Dobbs's plant will create a lot of jobs for the people who already live here, and it won't. My mom will make sure they know about that first thing tomorrow."

"That's fine if Mr. Lincoln and the council

want to keep Paradise Valley the way it is, but—what if they don't?" Jumping to her feet, Nicole began to pace like she always did when she was really agitated.

"They're elected to do what the people want, aren't they?" Ray fumed. "I just can't believe most of the people who live here want things to change as drastically as they're going to if Dobbs gets his way."

"Maybe, maybe not." Louis didn't waver when all heads turned to regard him as if he had just confessed to treason.

As Alex listened to his calm explanation, she realized Louis had a valid point. If he was serious, he would probably be an excellent lawyer.

"I'm being realistic. For all we know, most of the town's residents would rather have a chance to cash in on the development boom rather than preserve their small town lifestyle."

"Maybe," Nicole conceded. "But the city council isn't giving anyone an opportunity to decide what they want."

"Isn't there a law against that?" Ray asked.

"Not necessarily." Craig sighed. "My dad was telling me about a similar situation in a Kansas City suburb. People bought expensive houses in a new development with the understanding that the open land across the highway wouldn't be zoned for commercial use. The city council there okayed a major discount shopping center any-way—and got away with it even though the resi-dents tried to stop them."

Nicole exhaled with disgust. "The people in Paradise Valley can't try to stop something they don't know about."

"That's where Robyn comes in," Alex said.

Robyn looked up from her pad, her pen poised in midair. "Me?"

Alex nodded. "You've got a *Teen Take* TV seg-ment scheduled to air on the evening news to-morrow, don't you?"

"Yes, but even though I could probably tape some footage at the site and do a quick edit in the morning, broadcasting at six o'clock will be too late." Robyn frowned. "Won't it?"

"Seems to me," Alex pressed, "that this is so important, the news director at Channel Eleven might give you a spot on the noon edition."

"*Breaking News*, even," Ray added.

A slow smile lit up Robyn's face as she consid-ered her options. "I'm not sure *I* can get a *Break-ing News* spot, but Charlene Owens can. And I'm sure she'll put in a good word to get my segment aired early in exchange for the tip."

"And maybe Louis can go with you to speak for us," Alex suggested. "He can be pretty convincing."

"Okay by me," Louis said with a pleased smile. "I'll just pretend I'm giving a closing statement to the jury and winning or losing my case hangs in the balance."

"It does," Robyn observed somberly.

Louis got very serious very quickly. "Yeah, I know. It's a matter of life and death for Paradise Valley."

"Now we're getting somewhere." Nicole sat down again. "I know Robyn and Louis will be busy making the TV segment and the rest of us can't possibly cover the whole town, but we could still get enough signatures on a petition to add weight to the phone calls I just know are going to pour into City Hall."

"Count me in," Craig said.

"Me, too." Ray nodded.

"I'll write the petition tonight and print out a bunch of copies," Nicole said eagerly. "Can you all be here by eight tomorrow?"

Everyone gave Nicole a high five, but Alex opted out of the petition drive.

At eight o'clock tomorrow morning she would be camped out in Danielle Atron's outer office, where she would stay until the CEO of Paradise Valley Chemical agreed to see her.

"Do I look all right, Mom?" Standing in her mother's bedroom, Alex waited anxiously for the verdict. She had chosen the dark jacket and black pants from her limited business wardrobe. Whether or not Danielle Atron agreed to meet with her might hinge on making a favorable adult impression. Because she was the GC-161 kid the CEO of the chemical plant was looking for, she avoided having personal contact with Danielle whenever possible. Even so, Danielle knew she was George Mack's younger daughter and might not want to waste time visiting with one of her employee's kids.

"You look great. Very professional." Slipping on her shoes, Mrs. Mack eyed Alex with concern. "I still think I should talk to Danielle, though, Alex. She can be very difficult."

"No." Eyeing herself in the full-length mirror on the closet door, Alex tugged on her jacket sleeves and sighed. She had awakened her mother and father at six to fill them in on Mr. Dobbs's plans for Paradise Valley. Stunned, her father had agreed to drive her to Paradise Valley Chemical when he went to work.

Over Annie's objections, Alex thought with a smile. Now that her older sister was away at school most of the time, she had to learn to handle difficult problems on her own. So far, she was handling this one pretty well. Her parents obviously agreed. Without questioning that she had overheard Mr. Dobbs talking on his cell phone, her mom had rushed to get dressed so she could storm City Hall when it opened.

"You've got to talk to Mr. Lincoln and the city council as soon as possible, Mom."

"And hope I can talk some sense into them." Stepping behind Alex, Mrs. Mack gazed at her own reflection in the mirror and smoothed her hair. Then she smiled and put an arm around Alex's shoulders. "Well, win or lose, we make quite a team."

Although she was thrilled by her mom's acceptance of her as a professional equal, Alex's delight was dulled by the heavy burden of the circumstances. "Let's just hope we're a winning team."

Mrs. Mack's smile faded as she turned Alex to face her. "You've got to understand that in the real world, the good guys don't always win, Alex. All we can do is try."

"I know."

"Okay." Slinging her bag onto her shoulder, Mrs. Mack gestured toward the door. "Then let's get out there and give it our best shot."

And hope our best shot is good enough, Alex thought as they hurried down the stairs.

"Ready?" Mr. Mack downed his coffee and stood up from the kitchen table as Alex darted into the kitchen.

"As much as I'll ever be," Alex said. Her mother had gone out through the front and was already pulling out of the driveway.

Leaning against the counter, Annie sipped orange juice and stared at Alex over the rim of the glass. "Just how nervous are you about meeting with Danielle, Alex?"

Alex met her sister's pointed gaze. Having had a few unpleasant encounters with Danielle Atron during her brief internship at Paradise Valley Chemical, Annie was worried that Alex might start glowing under the pressure of a face-to-face discussion with the blunt and cunning CEO. Alex phrased her answer carefully. Her parents still didn't know she had been genetically altered by GC-161, or know about her unusual abilities. "Not *that* nervous."

"Let's go, Alex. I don't want to be late." Grabbing his portable computer and his briefcase, Mr. Mack hurried out the back door.

Settling into the front seat, Alex sighed heavily.

"I wish there was something more I could do to help," Mr. Mack said with genuine concern as he eased the car onto the road.

"Just be there for me when this is all over, okay, Dad? I may need a good, strong shoulder to cry on."

"You've got it." Smiling, Mr. Mack patted her knee. "But knowing you and your mother as well as I do, I've got a feeling we'll be celebrating instead."

Although pleased with the compliment, Alex wished she had as much confidence in herself as her dad did. When he drove off to the employee parking lot after dropping her in front of the PVC Administration Building, she was momentarily overwhelmed by how alone and vulnerable she felt. If Danielle did say or do something to make her really nervous, she would start to glow!

Taking several deep breaths, Alex pushed all thoughts of personal safety to the back of her mind and strode into the lobby intent on the business at hand—and *only* the business at hand.

The receptionist was pleasant and told her to have a seat after Alex asked to see Danielle on a matter of grave importance to the chemical company. The sterile atmosphere of the waiting area, which was created by black and chrome furniture broken only by the greens of a few tastefully arranged plants, was designed to intimidate. PVC's motto was written in raised block letters on the opposite wall.

Progress at Any Cost!

After staring at the phrase for a moment, Alex retreated into her own thoughts to offset the overpowering effects of the surroundings.

Progress.

Alex rolled the word over in her mind because it so aptly fit the problem in Paradise Valley. Progress was change and change was inevitable, but sudden, drastic change was not necessarily a good thing. Just as runaway change would ruin the town, Alex realized with a surge of insight, it could also be detrimental to people. And that applied to her and her friends. Their distinctive traits were the foundation of their unique and interesting personalities. Without them, everyone would be the same, with nothing to define their individual identities.

That explained why all her friends were reverting back to their basic natures even though they were trying hard not to. And that was just as well.

If Nicole hadn't trusted her instincts and questioned Mr. Dobbs's motives for wanting to build in Paradise Valley so rigorously, she might not have pursued trying to find out what his plans really were with such intensity.

Then they wouldn't know that Mr. Dobbs was plotting a one-man revolution to strip Paradise Valley of the distinctive qualities that set it apart from the hundreds of generic communities Craig had mentioned.

And that wasn't progress.

A counterrevolution was absolutely essential.

Latching onto Danielle Atron's own buzzword, Alex mentally rehearsed what she wanted to say to the CEO. Progress meant moving forward to something better, but in this situation, the meaning of better was different for everyone involved. However, the whole thing boiled down to more money for Mr. Dobbs and more tax revenues for the city or the preservation of Paradise

Valley's small-town identity. The real question was—how did Danielle Atron feel about it?

Alex was pretty sure she knew. Greed and power motivated the CEO.

With her confidence bolstered, sitting around waiting became intolerable. Taking another cue from Danielle, she decided that bold action was called for, and approached the receptionist's desk determined not to take no for an answer.

"I realize Ms. Atron is a very busy woman," Alex said politely but firmly. "However, I'm sure when she hears what I have to say, she'll be very glad she agreed to see me. Please, ask her again."

Barely hiding her irritation, the receptionist dialed. "I'm sorry to bother you again, Ms. Atron, but Ms. Mack insists on seeing you now. She says it's a matter of grave importance to the company."

Alex kept her expression composed despite the butterflies in her stomach when the receptionist nodded and looked up.

"She said, 'How grave can it possibly be?' "

"I suppose that depends on whether or not Ms. Atron wants to stop Dobbs Manufacturing from building a plant in Paradise Valley," Alex said evenly. Although she couldn't let the CEO know she knew about the PVC's top-secret and illegal experimental compounds like GC-161, she was counting on the fact that Danielle wanted to keep the town small and isolated. That was essential to minimizing the risk of having her illegal activities discovered. Combined with Danielle Atron's greed and desire to preserve her unchallenged position of power, Alex expected to get the CEO's full cooperation.

She was right.

The door into Ms. Atron's office opened before the receptionist could convey the message into the phone. Smiling, Danielle appeared and waved Alex inside. "Alex. Come in, come in. If I had known George Mack's daughter was here to see me, I wouldn't have kept you waiting so long."

Right, Alex thought. She smiled back. "Thank you."

Taking the chair Danielle indicated in front of her desk, Alex waited patiently until the CEO was seated and ready to talk.

"Now then, Alex." Clasping her hands, Danielle leaned across her desk expectantly. "Am I to understand that there's a way to stop Walter Dobbs from taking over my—the town?"

Ignoring the slip, Alex quickly recounted everything she had learned. As she talked, Danielle's expression went from attentive to appalled to furious.

"We're hoping," Alex concluded, "that the Channel Eleven news segments will rally the residents to put pressure on City Hall. However, that might not be enough to stop the process that's already been set in motion. However, it occurred to me that since *you* live here and want to keep Paradise Valley the way it is, too—"

"Oh, I do, I do." Danielle nodded sincerely without letting on that she had reasons entirely different from maintaining residential peace and tranquility.

Mentally rolling her eyes, Alex continued without a hint of her own feelings in her tone or manner. "Perhaps you could offer to buy Ordway's Range at a higher price. I know for a fact that the deal with Mr. Dobbs won't close until sometime this afternoon."

"That's it?" Danielle's temper flared, but she quickly regained her outward calm. Although there was a hard edge in her voice, her anger wasn't directed at Alex. "I've been *trying* to buy that property from Ordway for years to prevent *exactly* what's happening with Dobbs Manufacturing. That acreage is the only other property zoned for industrial use in Paradise Valley."

"Well, now that Mr. Ordway's decided to sell—"

"He won't sell to *me!*"

"Why not?" Alex asked before she could stop herself, and braced for a scathing retort that didn't come.

Sighing, Danielle shrugged. "I hired his daughter to work in the accounting department when the plant first opened, and fired her two weeks later because she thought software was an industry term for wardrobe. It took a week to get the department's computers back on-line and another week to enter all the data that were lost."

"Oh." Alex sagged as one of her best bets for beating Mr. Dobbs turned out to be a joker instead of an ace.

"I was perfectly justified, but Ordway's had a grudge against me ever since. However—" Staring thoughtfully at the ceiling, Danielle frowned. "Maybe there's a loophole that's been overlooked. I'll have my legal department look into it."

"I'll keep my fingers crossed." Rising, Alex extended her hand. "Thank you for your time anyway, Ms. Atron."

"You're quite welcome, Alex."

Cutting across the field beyond the plant to take a shortcut home, Alex felt good about how the interview had gone regardless of the disappointing results. She had done everything she could, and whatever happened with Dobbs Manufacturing now—happened. No matter what the outcome, she had taken on adult responsibilities and met them.

The trouble was, now she realized she wasn't quite so anxious to be an adult. She was barely halfway through her teenage years.

And she wasn't sure if she really wanted to spend her life as a public relations agent who had to resort to manipulation and compromise to get the job done even though those practices made her uncomfortable and didn't come naturally.

She certainly didn't want to spend one more day wearing clothes that were totally unsuitable to her real personality and normal activities.

And suddenly she didn't care if she broke her pre–New Year's resolution before midnight. Like the rest of her friends who couldn't help but return to their innate and wonderful, though slightly odd and unique personalities, she just wanted to be herself. The traits that needed to be modified would eventually resolve themselves with time and experience. That was what growing up was all about.

And she had plenty of time to decide what she wanted to do with her life, too. Right now, she just wanted to go to school, hang out with her friends, and be who she was.

Alex Mack: an ordinary kid with extraordinary powers.

There were a lot of ordinary kids in Paradise Valley who just wanted to be themselves, too! Alex ran down the far side of a small hill, anxious to act on another plan that had suddenly taken shape in her mind. With luck, she could activate the town's teen telephone network to correct another misguided mistake before it was too late.

Out of sight of the plant, Alex ducked into a small stand of trees and morphed—just because.

CHAPTER 12

Seated at the kitchen table with the cordless phone and the phone book, Alex dialed Cody Fancher. She got the answering machine and left a message.

"This is Alex Mack calling for Cody. I just wanted to let you know that there's been a change of plans for the New Year's Eve gala at the Community Center tonight. Wear whatever you want. Grub to formal—anything goes. And bring your favorite CD. Just don't forget to put your name on it. Thanks!"

Hanging up, Alex checked the time. It was eleven fifty-four and she was only up to the *F*s. Determined to cover as much territory as possible, she ran her finger down the listings until she hit a name she recognized. She had time for one more call before the noon edition of the Channel Eleven news started.

Linda Fenton was home and interrupted as soon as Alex started to explain her reason for calling.

"I already heard, Alex. Donna Bozgan called me about half an hour ago. Then I called Nora Clancy, but you had already reached her, so I called Tim Hursk."

"Great!" Alex wrote Tim's name on a blank sheet of paper so she wouldn't repeat the call.

"You don't know what a relief this is, Alex," Linda said with a long sigh. "My dad totally refused to let me get a formal gown and I wasn't going to come to the gala. Neither was Tim."

Alex blinked. She hadn't stopped to think that following so close after Christmas and the holiday expenses that strained many family budgets, a lot of kids wouldn't have been able to spend money on formal wear. Realizing that dispelled the lingering qualms she had about facing Kimberly when she arrived. The girl would not be pleased to find that the elegant dance she had hoped for had been changed back into a casual bash for a bunch of ordinary kids who wanted to dance to their own kind of music. How Kimberly felt was irrelevant, however. She didn't live in Paradise Valley.

On the other hand, Mrs. Lincoln had been understanding and cooperative when Alex had called to discuss the changes she wanted to make. Totally wrapped up in getting ready for the gala that night, the mayor's wife didn't seem to be aware of the other drama unfolding at City Hall. Her only concern was that the teenagers in town had a great time on New Year's Eve.

"Did Donna tell you to bring a CD?" Alex asked.

"Yeah, but I forgot to tell Tim."

"No problem. We'll have plenty."

After hanging up, Alex wrote down the title of Linda's CD. There were very few duplications. Ray and Louis still didn't have a clue that they were going to be recruited as the DJs, but she was sure they wouldn't refuse. And she didn't think her parents would object to donating the use of the family stereo. It was too late to cancel Chuck Cassidy's ballroom band, but Mrs. Lincoln had assured her the city would pay them if Mr. Dobbs decided not to. The band would play when the boys took their breaks, and under those circumstances, everyone would probably enjoy the old-fashioned big band sound. In fact, mingling the old and new music styles fit right in with the past and future decorating theme.

Taking the phone with her into the living room, Alex zapped on the TV. She settled back on the couch as the theme music for the noon news ended and Charlene Owens appeared.

"Good afternoon. Today in Washington, further allegations concerning the mismanagement—"

When the phone rang, Alex pushed the mute button but kept her eye glued to the screen. "Hello." It was her mother.

"I'm not having any luck down at City Hall, Alex. Do me a favor, will you?"

Alex could hear the frustration in her mom's voice. She had sounded much more confident earlier when she had called to brief her on the meeting with Danielle Atron. "Just tell me what."

"Throw a tape into the VCR and tape the noon news. I'll come home to pick it up in a little while."

Without hesitating, Alex telekinetically pulled a cassette off the stand and inserted it into the machine, then floated the remote over to the couch.

"If the city's phones start ringing off the hook this afternoon, I think our stubborn representatives might want to see what started all the ruckus."

Alex turned on the VCR and started the recording. "It's already done." Bidding her mom a quick good-bye, she hit the mute button to restore sound just as Charlene Owens shifted to local news.

"On the local scene, trouble may be brewing over the potential relocation of Dobbs Manufacturing to Paradise Valley. It is not known whether Mayor Lincoln and the city council are aware of Walter Dobbs's suspected intention to transfer all his existing personnel to the new facility, which would severely limit new jobs for current residents. It is also alleged that Mr. Dobbs plans to create a housing and commercial construction boom that would destroy the predominantly residential nature of the community."

Since the story was based on something Robyn had heard, and not on substantiated facts, the reporter was being careful not to openly accuse anyone of anything. That was okay. The broadcast would succeed if it got people to start asking questions and demanding answers.

"However," Ms. Owens continued, "little or no information has been made available to the public. We now switch you to Robyn Russo for a live edition of *Teen Take* on the proposed site."

"Yes!" A shiver of excitement raced up Alex's spine as the TV picture suddenly focused on Robyn and Louis standing in the middle of Ordway's Range. In a stroke of genius, Robyn had positioned herself so the giant town Christmas tree was visible in the background.

"This is Robyn Russo reporting from Ordway's Range which, as you can see, is situated right beside Paradise Valley Park. With me today is Louis Driscoll, a freshman at Paradise High."

Louis grinned self-consciously with a curt wave at the camera.

"As a teenaged resident of Paradise Valley, Louis, what's your opinion regarding the future development of our town if Dobbs Manufacturing moves in."

"I think allowing another major industry to build here would be a *big* mistake for a lot of reasons."

Alex grinned. Louis wasn't sticking to his resolution, either, which was probably fortunate. His blunt but honest opinion pretty much summed up how she and all her friends felt, and she was confident it would hit home with the voting adults in Paradise Valley, too.

"I can't speak for all the kids in town, but I'm sure my take on this reflects the feelings of most of them. For one thing, having a factory built right here where we're standing would totally ruin the quality of the park, not to mention the wildlife habitat that's developed on Ordway's Range over the years."

Alex wondered how many times Robyn and Louis had gone over the interview, then decided that that didn't matter, either. Even though it sounded rehearsed, they were touching on all the vital aspects of the Dobbs situation that the public needed to hear.

"What other effects do you think another industry would have on the town?" Robyn held the mike out.

"If that industry moved all its employees with it, there'd have to be more houses, more stores, more gas stations, and more and bigger highways to take care of the additional population. And Paradise Valley wouldn't be a quiet litle town that's a great place to live anymore. It would be gone like so many other small towns that get buried in suburban sprawl."

The camera zoomed in for a close-up on

Robyn. "In closing, I'd just like to add that kids don't have a voting say on important issues like deciding the fate of a town. Nevertheless, we do have an opinion because we live in Paradise Valley, too. This is Robyn Russo for Channel Eleven, signing off from Ordway's Range."

Alex hit the mute button again as the station broke for another commercial. Robyn and Louis had done a great job with the teen segment, and according to Nicole's eleven o'clock telephone report, the petition team was collecting signatures like crazy. Danielle Atron had been alerted and her mother was covering City Hall. All the wheels were in motion and there wasn't anything to do now but wait.

And make more phone calls.

CHAPTER 13

"That's it, Alex." Wearing jeans and a Grateful Dead T-shirt, Ray finished connecting both his own and the Macks' CD changers to the Community Center public address system. With two decks he could have a second CD cued up and waiting while another played. The few CDs Alex and Ray had brought were on the table between two microphones. "We're ready to rock and roll."

"Not without me, you're not."

Alex and Ray both looked around as Louis sauntered toward them. He was dressed in scuffed high-tops and jeans with a tear in one knee. However, they were topped off with a dress shirt that was unbuttoned at the neck and a tuxedo jacket that looked just a little too big.

"Couldn't decide what to wear, huh, Louis?" Ray quipped.

"Not at all, Ray," Louis retorted suavely. "Alex said 'grub to formal' and that's exactly what I've got on."

Alex laughed as she looked at Louis, then Ray. "Tux and tee. Works for me."

"How come your tux jacket's too big?" Ray asked.

"Because my mom bought it at a garage sale. The price was too good to pass up. I just never thought I'd ever have a reason to wear it." Shrugging, Louis glanced at Alex. "You're looking rather—"

"Ordinary?" Alex inserted for him.

"Yeah, but it isn't midnight yet and I didn't want to say so."

Alex just smiled. She had deliberately chosen to wear long denim coveralls with pink flowers embroidered on the bib and a plain white blouse. Boots and a blue denim hat with a short, up-turned brim and a pink artificial flower tucked into the hatband completed the Alex Mack look. It wasn't chic, but it was definitely her.

Sighing, Louis scanned the empty room. "It's awfully quiet in here."

"It's only quarter to eight. You guys can get started right after Chuck Cassidy finishes his sound check." Alex glanced toward the ten-piece band that was setting up on a second stage constructed of portable risers across the room. Mrs. Lincoln was talking with the leader. "I'll have Mr. Cassidy give you a high-five sign when he's done. I've got to find someone who knows how to turn down these lights."

Leaving the boys to sort through the CDs, Alex headed across the floor. Everything was ready and looked great.

The large black numbers sprinkled with silver glitter that marked the different years sparkled on the walls above groupings of photos and objects associated with each particular decade. Two long tables heaped with magazines covering a variety of topics, rolls of tape, and two dozen pairs of scissors stood at the end of the room opposite the entrance. Only the numbers denoting this and the next year hung high on the blank wall, which she hoped would be filled with clippings by the time the new year started. She had already decided what she wanted to put up and had the pictures stashed in her bag.

Surprisingly, the large round tables the Women's Auxiliary had arranged around the room near the walls looked wonderful, too. The white tablecloths added just a touch of elegance to the festive atmosphere. A bud vase with a single rose, a glass candle, a large bottle of nonalcoholic sparkling fruit drink, plastic champagne glasses, bags of confetti, noisemakers, and party hats sat in the center of each one. Extras of everything were stored in the far corner where the caterer was busy setting up the refreshment tables. A net full of colorful balloons which would be released at the stroke of midnight was secured to the ceiling.

If it wasn't for the uncertainty of the Dobbs Manufacturing situation, everything would be perfect.

Her mother had phoned at four o'clock to let her know that an emergency session of the city council had been called. The news coverage had had the desired effect. Not only were City Hall's phones ringing constantly, a lot of people had marched downtown to voice their protests in person. Alex hadn't heard a word since then.

Mrs. Lincoln glanced back as Alex came up behind her. "Looks like we're go for launch, Alexandra."

"And everything's A-okay." Alex smiled. "And just call me Alex."

"Okay. Did you need something?" Even though the mayor's wife was now aware of the Dobbs problem, she wasn't letting it interfere with the gala.

"Do you know how to work these lights?"

Nodding, Mrs. Lincoln left to adjust the lighting levels while Alex welcomed Chuck Cassidy, a spry man of sixty with a full head of gray hair and twinkling blue eyes. Since the band had been together for years and didn't rely on mega-electronics, the sound check would only take a few minutes. Alex was relieved to learn that Mr. Cassidy wasn't at all upset about playing second fiddle to two kids with CDs. It had been years since he and the other musicians had been able to relax and have fun on New Year's Eve.

As the track lights illuminating the walls turned on and the main lights dimmed, Alex saw Robyn and Nicole dash through the entrance and head straight to the restroom. Wondering if something was wrong, Alex ran after them.

". . . but you've got to promise not to tell Alex."

Robyn's voice stopped Alex just short of bursting through the restroom door.

"It can't be that awful," Nicole said.

"I just don't want to hurt her feelings." Robyn sighed. "Last night Craig told me that he flagged me down at the mall because he knew Alex and I were friends and he wanted to meet her."

"He was interested in Alex?" Nicole gasped.

Oh, no. Alex tensed, then relaxed as Robyn finished explaining.

"Yeah, but only until we started talking and found out how much alike we are." Robyn laughed. "The really funny thing is that if I hadn't decided to assume the best instead of the worst when Craig first talked to me, I probably would have said or done something to spoil everything!"

"Chalk up one for the power of positive thinking." Nicole hesitated. "But keep in mind that sometimes it's not a bad thing to assume the worst, either. Like with Kimberly and her father."

"Gotcha. If you want to know the truth, I didn't stop thinking the worst. I just stopped talking about it."

Alex scurried backward as the door suddenly opened and both girls stepped out. Robyn was wearing a short black velvet dress with ankle boots. Nicole had on a long dark green skirt and a short-sleeved, cream-colored sweater. The scooped neckline was accented with sequins.

"Hey, Alex!" Robyn nervously avoided looking at her.

"I wondered where you had disappeared to," Alex said casually. "I saw you come in and then you vanished."

"Just had some last minute primping to do!" Nicole smiled tightly.

Robyn relaxed, then waved wildly as Craig stepped clear of the crowd of kids streaming into the hall. The manner of dress ranged from jeans and tees like Ray to conservatively dressed up like Nicole. "Craig! Over here!"

Across the room, Alex saw Chuck Cassidy put down his trumpet and give the anxious young DJs a thumbs-up. Exchanging a totally delighted look with Louis, Ray pressed a button on the CD changer. "The Time Warp" from *The Rocky Horror Picture Show* suddenly blared through the PA speakers mounted in all four corners.

Perfect.

"It's party time!" Slipping his arm around Robyn, Craig bowed slightly to Nicole and Alex. He looked super in gray slacks and a navy blue blazer.

Nicole sighed. "Yeah. I just wish we knew for

sure if we had something to celebrate. Have you heard anything from your mom about what's going on at City Hall, Alex?"

"Not since they called that emergency meeting of the city council." Looking past Craig's shoulder, Alex saw Kelly and Stacy walk in and stop dead with horrified gasps.

Wearing a long, royal blue, formal gown, Kelly sputtered. "What's going on here? I thought this was supposed to be formal?"

"It was," Stacy said, turning pale as she realized she was way overdressed in a floor-length red taffeta gown with long white evening gloves.

"Oops." Alex winced. She had left messages on both girls' answering machines, but they had obviously not listened to them. Quickly recovering from their initial shock, Kelly and Stacy defiantly lifted their chins and glided gracefully across the floor to commandeer an empty table.

Kimberly, however, was infinitely less accepting and much more vocal about the last-minute change in dress code.

Laughing as she entered the hall with her father, Kimberly stopped dead just inside the entrance and gasped. Her eyes widened as she scanned the room and her face reddened with furious indignation.

Taking a deep breath, Alex walked over to greet them. Robyn, Craig, and Nicole followed but hung back as Kimberly lashed out.

"This is outrageous!" Fuming, Kimberly glared at Alex. Although she looked like a New York model in a long, sleek gold gown that fell in soft folds at the neck and from her hips to the floor, the dark anger that twisted her pretty face totally destroyed any essence of class she had hoped to achieve. "How could you do this to me, Alex? Everyone's dressed like they just walked in off the street! And you look like a hillbilly teeny-bopper!"

Alex's only facial response was a slight smile. "Actually, this is how I look most of the time, Kimberly. And I didn't do anything to you. In fact, I almost let you do something to me. To all of us."

Catching a fisted gesture of encouragement from Nicole, Alex continued calmly. "This is a Paradise Valley party, Kimberly, and this is what Paradise Valley kids are really like."

"Well, I think you're all disgusting."

"Kimberly!" Mr. Dobbs said sharply. "Behave yourself. These young people may be your only source of friends soon."

"I don't think so!" Dark eyes ablaze with indignation, Kimberly glared at her father. "I will not live in this—this village!"

"You will not have a choice," Mr. Dobbs said sternly. "I've bought the land and that's that. You've got to remember that change takes time—"

"But there won't be any changes in this town anytime soon." A man's baritone voice interrupted.

All heads turned and Alex tensed as the mayor, her mother, a member of the city council, and Danielle Atron entered. Spotting her distinguished looking husband, Valerie Lincoln rushed over to join them.

"It's my pleasure as mayor of Paradise Valley," Mr. Lincoln went on, "to inform you that the property you purchased this afternoon, Mr. Dobbs, has been rezoned for residential use only. Effective at seven fifty-six P.M. this evening."

"You can't do that!" Mr. Dobbs exploded with an anger that exceeded Kimberly's.

His daughter blinked, then sagged in relief. Since her father's industry wouldn't be moving to Paradise Valley, neither would she.

"Oh, yes, we can." The mayor smiled.

"Especially if we want to get reelected," the councilman added with an emphatic nod.

"And what am I supposed to do with acres of worthless property?" Mr. Dobbs demanded.

Mrs. Mack stepped forward. "I think we have a solution you'll find satisfactory. I'd like you to meet—"

"Danielle Atron." Not one to mince words or waste time, Danielle planted herself in front of Mr. Dobbs and looked him straight in the eye. "I'll buy that property for *exactly* what you paid for it this afternoon."

Startled, Mr. Dobbs hesitated before he extended his hand. "You've got a deal, Ms. Atron." Then to everyone's surprise, including Kimberly's, he smiled. "I know when I'm beaten and I prefer to lose as graciously as I win."

"Which is greatly appreciated, believe me." The mayor looked at Danielle expectantly. "Didn't you have something to add, Ms. Atron?"

Alex sensed that everyone around her was bursting to shout with joy. However, they all held back, waiting to see what the CEO of Paradise Valley Chemical had to say.

"As a concerned citizen," Ms. Atron said, forcing a phony smile. "I've decided to donate Atron's Range to the city as a permanent wildlife preserve and extension of the park."

"Yes!" Nicole whooped with joy.

Applause, whistles, and cheers rose above the music as everyone nearby joined in whether or not they knew what had just transpired.

Alex sighed as Danielle's face clouded. She was obviously not happy about giving away a valuable piece of property.

Taking Alex aside, Mrs. Mack grabbed her by the shoulders and started jumping up and down. "We did it!"

Laughing, Alex bounced up and down with her until her mother calmed down.

"It feels great to save a town, doesn't it?"

"Yes," Alex agreed. "But how did you ever convince Danielle to give all that land to Paradise Valley?"

"That was easy. The city council wouldn't agree to rezone to keep Dobbs Manufacturing from building on it unless she did."

"What if she had said no?" Alex asked aghast.

Mrs. Mack smiled smugly. "They were just bluffing, but she didn't dare call them on it. As far as she knew, it was the only way to keep Dobbs out. Just as we suspected, keeping her undisputed position of power was worth more than keeping a property the city wouldn't let her build on, either."

Alex nodded with supreme satisfaction as the

mayor called her mother back to celebrate with the adults in an adjoining room. Mr. Dobbs went with them, leaving Kimberly standing in the doorway. Feeling sorry for her, Alex went over.

"Come on, Kimberly. Lighten up."

Kimberly frowned uncertainly.

Alex smiled. "You might as well relax and try to have a good time with us tonight. Who knows? You might even enjoy yourself."

"I doubt it." Kimberly pouted as she met Alex's sincere gaze, then shrugged. "But I don't have anything better to do. Where's Ray?"

"He's busy."

A good-looking junior who played hockey and looked totally uncomfortable in his black tuxedo came up to Kimberly and smiled shyly. "Would you like to dance?"

"Why not?" Looking bored but resigned, Kimberly took his hand and let him lead her to the dance floor.

Left alone in the entrance as everyone else flung themselves into the festivities, Alex took a moment to catch her breath. It had been a long, hard week, but worth every ounce of energy she had put into it. No one would have to worry about Paradise Valley turning into a modern-day boomtown again. And her career essay for English was as good as written. It wouldn't take any time at all to write five hundred words on why she *didn't* want to work in the field of public relations.

And with all that settled, Alex decided, it was time to join in the fun. The next few hours passed in a whirl of dancing with anyone who asked, talking with everyone she knew and having a total blast.

When Ray joined Alex at the "this year/next year" wall, she looked at him curiously. "How come you're taking a break now? It's almost midnight."

"Louis and I decided to let Chuck emcee in the new year. He's had a lot of practice and we don't want to miss a chance to go totally crazy with everyone else. What are you doing?"

"Getting ready to make my contribution to this wall—if I can find room." Holding her pictures and two strips of tape, Alex shrugged. The project had been a huge success and the entire surface within reach was covered with magazine photos that depicted everything from sporting events to school activities, social and political issues, and everyday life.

"Just put them anywhere, Alex. The countdown's gonna start any second."

"Okay." Choosing spots just off the centerline on both sides, Alex taped her current school picture on the "this year" side and an identical copy on the "next year" panel.

"They're both the same?" Ray frowned. "How come?"

"Because I'll always be just me. I don't mean that I won't change as time goes by. I will. But from now on, I'm going to be true to myself regardless of what anyone else thinks."

"Me, too. High finance is out. DJ is in. At least, for now." Ray laughed. "And for the record, I think you're pretty terrific, Alex."

"So are you, Ray."

"Ten!" Chuck Cassidy boomed through his mike.

The crowd shouted. "Nine, eight, seven—"

"Six, five—" Alex saw one of her pictures start to slip as she and Ray joined in. She pressed it back up with a telekinetic push and grinned, happy with herself and the world. "Two, one!"

"Happy New Year!"

About the Author

Diana G. Gallagher lives in Minnesota with her husband, Marty Burke, three dogs, three cats, and a cranky parrot. When she's not writing, she likes to read, walk the dogs, and look for cool stuff at garage sales for her grandsons, Jonathan, Alan, and Joseph.

Diana and Marty are musicians who perform traditional and original Irish and American folk music at coffeehouses and conventions around the country. Marty sings and plays the twelve-string guitar and banjo. In addition to singing backup harmonies, Diana plays rhythm guitar and a round Celtic drum called a *bodhran*.

A Hugo Award–winning artist, Diana is best known for her series *Woof: The House Dragon*. Her first adult novel, *The Alien Dark*, appeared in 1990. She and Marty coauthored *The Chance Factor*, a STARFLEET ACADEMY VOYAGER book. In addition to other STAR TREK novels for intermediate readers, Diana has written many books in other series published by Minstrel Books, including *The Secret World of Alex Mack*, *Are You Afraid of the Dark*, and *The Mystery Files of Shelby Woo*. She is currently working on original young adult novels for the Archway Paperback series *Sabrina, the Teenage Witch*.

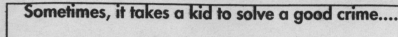

Have you ever wished for the complete guide to surviving your teenage years? At long last, here's your owner's manual—a book of instructions and insights into exactly how YOU operate.

Let's Talk About Me!

A Girl's Personal, Private, and Portable Instruction Book for life

Learn what makes boys so weird
Discover the hidden meanings in your doodles
Uncover the person you want to be
Get to know yourself better than anyone else on Earth
Laugh a little
Think a little
Grow a little

Top-Secret Quizzes, Cool Activities, and Much, Much More

Being a teenage girl
has never been so much fun!

**From the creators of
the bestselling CD-ROM!**

An Archway Paperback
Published by Pocket Books

1384-01

NANCY DREW® MYSTERY STORIES By Carolyn Keene